"Darien Gee reminds us of the true spirit of the season. A lovely read." —Lynne Branard, *The Art of Arranging Flowers*

"Fans of women's food-and-crafting fiction will relish these stories...[the] 'pay it forward' message is appropriate any time of year." —*Kirkus Reviews*

"Tales of quiet transformation." —*Chico News and Review*

"A lovely Christmas book...filled with heartwarming tales that are perfect for the Christmas season." —*Mysteries Etc.*

Praise for
THE AVALON LADIES SCRAPBOOKING SOCIETY

"A welcome addition to any women's-fiction collection." —*Booklist*

"A three-hanky nod to *It's a Wonderful Life*. Gee—who also writes as Mia King (*Table Manners*)—gets the unapologetically schmaltzy tone just right with the irresistible premise that we can love the impossible. A surefire book club hit." —*Publisher's Weekly*

"Poignant and memorable...a gratifying read." —*Huffington Post*

"In this exceptionally well-written novel you'll find heartwarming inspiration, humor, wisdom and endless charm...This is one of those books you'll want to tell your friends...Gee is an author to keep a close eye on." —*RT Book Reviews*

"In a gathering of women there will always be compelling stories. There are shared secrets, support, encouragement, and love as the women of *The Avalon Ladies Scrapbooking Society* come to terms with the past and boldly step forward into the future."
—Debbie Macomber, *New York Times* bestselling author

"Truly charming! Darien Gee writes about friendship and family with depth, grace and heart."
—Sarah Jio, *New York Times* bestselling author

"Darien Gee pieces together lives and scraps with the skill and heart of a true storyteller. I loved it!"

—Lisa Wingate, national bestselling author

AN AVALON
CHRISTMAS

DARIEN GEE

ALSO BY DARIEN GEE

Fiction
An Avalon Christmas
The Avalon Ladies Scrapbooking Society
Friendship Bread

Nonfiction
Writing the Hawai'i Memoir

WRITTEN AS MIA KING

Table Manners
Sweet Life
Good Things

AN AVALON
CHRISTMAS

Library of Congress Cataloging-in-Publication Data
Gee, Darien.
An Avalon Christmas: a novel / Darien Gee.
p. cm.
1. City and town life—Illinois—Fiction. 2. Female Friendship—Fiction 3. Christmas stories. I. Title.
2014903385

Published in the United States of America

ISBN 978-0-97543163-4
eISBN 978-0-97543162-7

2 4 6 8 9 7 5 3 1

Cover design by Matthew Pearce

Dedicated to Nancy Sue Martin,
a dear friend who embodies the spirit of giving
and sharing with others every single day

*Pleasure is spread through the earth
in stray gifts to be claimed by whoever shall find.*

WILLIAM WORDSWORTH

Lemon Creams

MELVIN O'MALLEY IS READING the paper when Mary McLean, one of the certified nurse aides, knocks on the open door of his room. In front of her is an empty wheelchair.

"I hope that's not for me," Melvin says dryly, not looking up. He removes the Arts and Entertainment section and folds it lengthwise, careful to crease the paper evenly down the middle. It's an old habit from his commuting days, where he'd ride the train for an hour, cramped for space. Everyone did that back then, fold the paper into quadrants and read it section by section. He takes a sip of his coffee and pretends to keep reading.

"Not yet," Mary says, smiling sweetly. "But if you don't get up and get some exercise, I may be pushing you around like Mr. Peterson."

Clark Peterson lives in the room adjacent to Melvin. He spends his days in bed watching television except when Mary can cajole him into taking a spin around the grounds in the wheelchair. Melvin doesn't know why she insists on taking Old Peterson out (he's actually two years younger than Melvin, a fact Melvin finds disturbing)—it's not like he's training to run the marathon. He's waiting for the inevitable, like all of them.

"I already did my walk this morning," Melvin informs her with a snap of his paper. "Half a mile."

"Then it won't kill you to take a walk to the common room…" Mary continues. Her eyes light up in excitement. "Because it's time for the holiday exchange!"

"No, thank you."

"Every participating resident is guaranteed a present," she says. "Aren't you the least bit curious?"

"Nope."

"Last year Eunice Weeks got a handheld sewing machine worth eighty dollars."

"And she sewed Ron Taylor into his bed while he was asleep." Ron almost fell out of bed the next morning as he struggled with his sheets. Ron's daughter had been furious when she found out, threatening to sue Harmony Homes.

Mary's smile doesn't waver. "That was just a lover's spat," she says dismissively. "But what about Mrs. Shadle? A one-year membership to the fruit of the month club!"

"I hate fruit."

"I'm just saying that there are some nice big ticket items under the tree. The rest are all small things, but very nice, I'm told. Come on, Melvin. It'll be fun, I promise!" She's begging him. No wonder Clark Peterson lets her push him around in the wheelchair. It's easier just to give in than to argue.

The truth is, Melvin likes Mary. She's a spry little thing with a blond pixie haircut and clear sparkly nail polish. She joined the staff at Harmony Homes a year ago and she's a breath of fresh air compared to the dour-looking folks who run this place. She's too young to know any better, still in her twenties, all full of optimism and cheer. He'd be annoyed if she weren't so damn nice.

He stares into Mary's hopeful face and for a second actually considers going. But Melvin hates any sort of group activity, even eating in the dining room. It's bad enough that he's here, surrounded by geriatrics who can't take care of themselves or who forget their own name. The only thing they have in common is that they've all been abandoned by their kids. Kids with their own lives, too busy to care for their aging parents.

"Don't let me get in the way," he'd said sarcastically when his own daughter, Barbara, showed him the brochures. He glanced at the glossy pictures of smiling seniors, their hair washed and perfectly coiffed, their clothes clean and pressed. The reality? With the exception of himself and a handful of others, nobody else seems to own so much as a comb. A few people wear their clothes inside out, and many just stay in their robes all day. Nobody plays bocci ball or swings a golf club on the executive putting course out back. Nobody takes salsa classes or learns to cook Thai food.

"Dad, you can't live by yourself anymore," Barbara had tried to explain. This was happening because he'd almost hit someone with his car. It was an accident. And leaving the stove on. Another accident. But throwing a brick through his neighbor's window after her designer-bred poodle, something called a Labradoodle, left a trail of soft dog poop by his Japanese maple…well, he told the police it was an accident, but he and the Labradoodle know better. Melvin chuckles at the memory.

"So, what'll it be, Melvin? I have to go get Mr. Peterson. He heard there's a miniature snooker set and he's anxious to get a good seat." Mary drums her sparkly nails against the handles of the wheelchair, feigning impatience, but Melvin knows she's teasing him.

"Maybe next year," he says.

There's a flash of disappointment in her eyes, but a

second later she's smiling again. "Okey dokey," she says gamely, then waves as she walks past his doorway. "See you later!"

Melvin sighs and turns his attention back to his paper, his eyes focusing on the small headline in front of him. EXPRESS YOURSELF! OPEN MIC NIGHTS GROW IN POPULARITY ACROSS THE COUNTRY.

What a load of rubbish. Melvin frowns as he skips to the next article, something about a new exhibit at the Art Institute of Chicago. He wouldn't mind seeing it if Barbara could find the time to take him. But she's divorced with two spoiled kids and a sanctimonious ex-husband and alimony. Melvin doesn't understand how a woman who doesn't work won't let her dad take up residence in one of the many guest rooms in her house. True, they've never been very close and he was always busy at work, and maybe his own bitter divorce from Barbara's mother may have jaded her somewhat, but still.

There's the sound of someone shuffling by in their slippers. Melvin doesn't look up, but he sees the nappy pink bathrobe from the corner of his eye. He tries to duck behind the paper but it's too late.

"Mel-vin, yoo hoo!" comes a delighted cry from the hallway. There's a *shuffle-shuffle-shuffle* as Alice Edwidge turns ninety degrees and makes her way towards Melvin, going all of one mile per hour as she pushes forward on her walker. The sight of the yellow tennis balls, their neon sheen dull and fuzzy as they scoot closer towards him, makes him shake his head. Really? Tennis balls? Gilbert Hobbs has something that looks like miniature skis on his, and Franco Juarez has some high-tech digital device that beeps if you go too fast or near an obstacle. Ridiculous, in Melvin's opinion. If he ever ends up needing a walker, so help him God, Melvin's going to find the highest hill and release the brakes.

See ya.

Alice Edwidge is in his room now, beaming as she approaches, her face wrinkled and earnest. Her lips are painted a bold, pouty red. Mary McLean's doing, no doubt.

"Hello, Mrs. Edwidge," Melvin says reluctantly. He puts down his paper.

She bats her lashes as she leans on her walker, slightly out of breath. "Call me Alice," she scolds him. "Or Allie. That was my nickname."

"Yes, ma'am."

"*Ma'am?* You're making me feel so old!" She casts a watery glance around his room. It's a one-bedroom with a small living area, which he's sitting in now. She peers just beyond him into the bedroom, gives a small nod of approval. "You're a very neat man, Melvin. I like that. My late husband was like that. Into hospital corners and everything. You like hospital corners?"

Melvin sighs. All he wants is to be left alone, to be able to read his paper and have his cup of coffee, to listen to the morning program on public radio. But these mandatory open door hours—one hour in the morning, one hour in the afternoon, one hour in the evening—which the administration likes to refer to as "promoting communication, connection and interaction" among Harmony Home residents, is a farce. Melvin suspects it's a quick and easy way to make sure nobody's croaked in their bed, a five-second glance down the hallways to make sure everyone is present and accounted for.

"I like hospital corners just fine," he says. His bed sheets are so tight you could bounce a quarter on them. Eighteen inches from head to fold, no wrinkles. The trick is to start making your bed while you're still in it.

"I haven't made my bed in years," Alice tells him. "Between the arthritis and my lack of good muscle tone, it's a miracle I'm even walking." She pats the walker. "Well, with the help of ol' Charlie here. Don't know what I would have done without him."

Despite himself, Melvin feels a smile tugging at the corners of his mouth as he stares at the beat-up walker, scratched and dented up and down the legs. "Charlie?" he asks.

Alice looks appalled. "Don't tell me I never introduced you to Charlie! He's a lifesaver. I wouldn't be out and about if it wasn't for Charlie."

Melvin is about to ask more when Mary McLean appears in the doorway.

"There you are, Alice!" she says with relief. "We're starting the holiday exchange. Don't you want to join us?"

For a second the smile seems frozen on Alice's face, replaced by a look of confusion. She turns to Melvin. "I don't know. Do I? What were we talking about?" There's a slight tremor in her voice.

Melvin knows Mary's watching him. He also knows that Alice Edwidge has moments like this, moments where she gets lost. "We were talking about going to the common room," he says, standing up. "I'll escort you."

Alice beams, back to her old self. "Oh, yes! That's right!" She grunts as she turns her walker around towards the door and begins to edge forward. "Let's go!"

Mary waits for them to pass her, grinning at Melvin like a Cheshire cat.

"It was time for my morning exercise anyway," he informs her shortly.

"But I thought you already walked half a mile," she says, feigning innocence.

Melvin just gives her an annoyed look.

It takes them a while to get to the common room. Alice slows down every few feet to talk to any lingering residents, tries to convince them to join the holiday exchange. After a few minutes Melvin feels a bit like the Pied Piper, a small entourage of octogenarians following them down the hall.

When they finally get there, Melvin is surprised to see that the room is packed. Wheelchairs are lined against the wall, people sitting in every available space on the couches and chairs. Red and green paper chains drape from the ceiling along with paper snowflakes and signs that say JOY and FA LA LA LA LA. Christmas music is being piped in over the loudspeakers. Bing Crosby, one of Melvin's favorites.

Melvin hasn't seen this many residents in one place for a long time. Fourth of July will draw a crowd because of the firework display, as will Easter with the ridiculous golden egg hunt (whoever finds it gets a double helping of dessert for a month). Birthdays pull in a few extra people, too, mostly those wanting a piece of cake or hoping for a go at the presents when the birthday girl or boy isn't looking. Thanksgiving was painful, with the staff dressed as pilgrims, wicker cornucopias filled with plastic fruit on every table. Barbara and the kids had insisted on coming here for turkey instead of inviting him back to her house for the holidays, which Melvin thought was odd. She's already told him that Christmas is a busy time for her, that she has something special planned for the kids at Disneyland or some place out west, so he's not even sure if he'll be seeing her.

The room is warm. Mary spent most of the morning corralling people into the common room and some of them have fallen asleep, bored with the waiting. But quite a few have come in on their own accord, their eyes fixed hungrily on the center of the room where a large fake Christmas tree is decorated with wooden popsicle ornaments from the afternoon crafts class.

Stacks of presents are wrapped in colorful foil paper and festive holiday prints beneath the tree. They've had holiday exchanges in the past, but the presents were always small—one year they each received a roll of Lifesavers, a gift Melvin found ironic if you thought about it. But this year, looking at the bounty underneath the Christmas tree, Melvin has to admit it's an impressive collection.

"All right, everybody!" Mary claps her hands together, and some people begin clapping along with her, thinking it's a game. Melvin helps Alice into a chair and positions himself against the wall, near the exit. Just in case.

"Mr. Jenks, can you please turn down the music? Thank you. If everyone is ready, it's time for our holiday exchange!" Mary makes her way to the center of the room, smiling sweetly and patting people on the shoulder as she passes them.

Melvin gives her six more months, maybe a year at best. He hasn't been here all that long but already he's seen most of the staff at Harmony Homes come and go. Those who do this as a career get bored and look for new opportunities, bouncing from one facility to another and sometimes back again. Those who come in bright-eyed and bushy-tailed, like Mary, tend to get disillusioned and discouraged. Their big ideas, their enthusiasm, get tamped down like a stake in the ground. Because let's face it—this isn't Disneyland. This is where people come to die. It's a kind of purgatory, because the really sick folks aren't here, just people who are aging who have no one to look after them. Melvin has already been here three years, and knows with his life expectancy, he could be here for another ten.

"Now, everyone's name is in this box." Mary pulls out a box from under the tree, and Melvin can see it's different from the rest. It's unwrapped, a simple pine box with a lid. The only decoration is a bright red bow glued on the front. Mary removes the lid. "When I call your name, you can come up and pick a present. If you want me to pick a present for you, just raise your hand and either me or Daryl will bring it to you. Ready?"

There's more interest now, and even Melvin feels himself leaning forward. He's scanning the presents, noticing that no two presents are alike, either in size or the wrapping paper. Hmm, that's interesting. Last year everything was wrapped in one of three papers—a snowman motif, a Christmas tree motif, and one that was filled with multicolored balls, a generic paper that was probably borrowed from the birthday stash.

"Okay, first name!" Mary reaches into the box, pulls out a small strip of paper. "Lottie Rush!"

There's a squeal as heads turn. Lottie Rush, a spry African American woman in her eighties, jumps out of her chair. She's wearing yoga pants and a baggy t-shirt that used to belong to her husband. She races to the center of the room.

"Just one, Lottie," Mary reminds her as Lottie's arms start filling up with presents. After a few seconds of gentle encouragement, Lottie releases the other presents and returns to her seat with a large box. The minute she sits down she starts ripping off the paper.

"A Thigh Toner!" she exclaims, holding the box over her head. "It's exactly what I wanted!"

There's a smattering of applause as all heads turn back to Mary. Mary smiles and reaches into the box again.

"Alfonzo Owens!" she calls.

Alfonzo raises his cane.

"Okey dokey, I'll pull one for you." Mary turns and stares at the pile. "You like green, right?"

A nod. Alfonzo had his voice box taken out after being diagnosed with advanced pharyngeal cancer. He has a small box that he presses against his throat when he wants to be heard, but Alfonzo finds it easier to communicate in other ways. Melvin gets the sense that he was never much of a talker to begin with.

Mary reaches in and plucks out a long box wrapped in green foil paper. Daryl, the other nurse's aide, takes it back to Alfonzo. Alfonzo unwraps the paper with shaky hands, a sign of early Parkinson's. There's a murmur from the men around him when they see what he has. Alfonzo shakes his cane in triumph.

"Lucky bastard," Melvin hears one man muttering to his friend. "That has a double flex rod with an automatic anti-reverse."

"Looks like it came with a mini tackle box, too," his friend says. "And two bonus lures!"

Melvin remembers that Alfonzo was—is—an avid fisherman. He watches as a few men shuffle over from across the room to inspect Alfonzo's gift.

"Leah Casey, you're next," Mary calls out.

Melvin can feel Alice fretting next to him. "I do hope all the good presents don't go first," she says. "Last year I got a shoe shine kit. Traded it for a marble rolling pin, but I can't even lift it." She shakes her head.

Melvin can't think of anything reassuring to say. If it were anybody else, he'd tell them that honest truth—you get what you get. But watching Alice Edwidge eye the presents anxiously, he sees that her lipstick is already starting to feather and that she's wringing her hands in worry. He feels himself reach out and pat her on the back.

Mary's picking up the pace now, calling out names and ushering presents into the right hands or waving people to come forward.

"Arline Herring, come on down!"

"Madge Bennett!"

"Calling Ethel Montgomery!"

"Brent Stout, it's your turn!"

Melvin feels himself dozing off. It's the heat of the room, too many bodies, the thermostat already five degrees higher than it needs to be. Outside the December day is grey and listless, no snow on the ground, everything bare and colorless.

"Clark Peterson!"

Hearing his neighbor's name, Melvin opens one eye. He sees Clark Peterson insist that Daryl take him up to the front in the wheelchair. It's the most lively he's seen the old boy in days.

It takes some maneuvering, but Daryl manages to get the wheelchair through the crowded room to the Christmas tree. About half of the presents are left. Clark screws up his face, concentrating on each present as if he can see through the wrapping. Some residents are getting antsy, ready to charge the tree or just head back to their rooms. Marcelo Nielsen, 83, breaks out into "The Art of the Possible" from Evita. Clark finally plucks a present from under the tree.

As Daryl wheels him back, Clark is ripping off the paper like a kid on Christmas morning. He lets out a whoop and holds a miniature snooker set over his head. "Eight ball in the corner pocket!" he hollers with more gusto than Melvin has even seen. Mary is laughing then dips her hand into the box to pull out the next name.

"Oh," Alice says again, wringing her hands. "It looks like everyone's getting what they want. That's good, right?"

Melvin considers this. Clark with his snooker set, Alfonzo with his fishing rod. Lottie with her thigh toner, which she's already taken out of the box and is using with a little too much enthusiasm. Leah with a perfumed stationary set, Madge with a telephone that has pockets for pictures of each of her grandkids. Arline got a trio of succulent plants. Ethel, a former beautician, has a decorative jar filled with hair ties. Brent received a retractable umbrella with his alma mater's logo. Granted, a handful of residents attended the University of Chicago, but still it's a funny coincidence.

Melvin watches as three more residents go up and choose a gift, each one reacting with surprise and joy. At their age, they're beyond niceties and polite platitudes—if they don't like something, they say so. But so far everyone seems delighted, a far cry from year's past and suspicious as far as Melvin's concerned.

It's Mary, it has to be. In the short time she's been here, she's taken the time to get to know everyone intimately, knows their stories, their histories. Of course she would know what they want for Christmas.

"Thank you, Mary, but I'm Jewish," Ella Steiner informs Mary when her name is called. "I told Daryl it was unnecessary for me to come, but he insisted." She wrinkles her nose and pretends to give Daryl an exasperated look, but he just smiles and waves.

"Isn't today the fifth day of Hanukkah?" Mary asks.

Ella nods. "It is."

"Well, you are welcome to choose a gift in the spirit of the holidays," Mary continues, "but if you'd rather not, I understand. We do our best to make this a festive time, celebrating all faiths, but I know we fall short. I'm sorry, Ella."

Ella considers this, then nods. "Well, why not?" She stands up gracefully, brushing imaginary lint from her pantsuit. Melvin tries to remember her situation as she makes her way to the center of the room. Her story is a bit like his, with children too busy living their own lives. She's younger than most of the people here, in her early seventies, a widow.

Ella approaches the tree carefully, almost warily. He's seen her help other residents with a stealthy kindness, refusing any acknowledgment, but her generosity intrigues him. After a moment's hesitation, she reaches for a gift wrapped in a simple blue paper. "I'll open this in my room," she tells Mary. "Thank you."

Mary calls out a few more names, and the presents start to dwindle under the tree. Alice Edwidge is beside herself, almost in tears.

"Alice," Mary calls out, reading from the strip of paper in her hand. "Alice Edwidge!"

"It's me!" Alice turns to Melvin. "Finally!" She grips her walker and starts moving forward, eyes shining.

The next moment happens in slow motion. Too many people in the room, maybe, or perhaps Alice's own excitement had gotten the better of her. Later, Melvin will notice that all the tennis balls on Harmony Homes' walkers will be replaced with generic plastic sliders.

The walker tips, snagged on something invisible, and Alice goes with it, a fragile porcelain doll. At first the fall seems of no consequence, nothing more than a snowflake drifting lazily towards the ground. Someone will grab hold of her, or perhaps she'll regain her balance, admonishing herself later for her own clumsiness.

But none of that happens. When Alice lands, she lands harder than it would seem possible. There's a crack followed by a dull thud. For a second the room is silent.

And then Daryl and Mary are rushing forward, more aides coming in from the hallway, the kitchen. Sudden commotion, pandemonium. Someone is on the phone. Residents are wailing, some are observing, and others are trying to console their friends.

In a matter of minutes everyone is ushered back to their rooms. Melvin himself is unclear as to how he got back there. One moment he was in the common room, the next he is sitting on his bed in a daze.

The morning sun becomes the noon sun becomes the

afternoon sun. Melvin sits, and waits.

At last there's a gentle knock on his door. "Melvin?"

It's Mary McLean. Her eyes are red and puffy, her face sallow. She comes in and sits next to him on the bed.

"Mrs. Edwidge is over at the hospital in Freeport," she tells him, touching him on the arm. "I don't know what's going to happen. I'm sorry, Melvin." She sniffs.

Melvin wants to tell her that he hardly knows Alice Edwidge, that her condolences are misplaced. Elden Burns, he wants to say. They would often sit together, giggling like school children. Go tell Elden, he wants to say.

But Mary just edges closer, puts an arm around his shoulder. From her sweater pocket she produces a square box, wrapped in silver paper. "We didn't get to finish the holiday gift exchange," she says in a quiet voice. "But I think this one is for you." When he doesn't move to take it, she places it on the nightstand table.

"Buzz us if you need anything," she tells him. She stands up, places her hand on his shoulder again. This time, he reaches up and rests his hand on hers. A sob bubbles up in his chest, and a second later he's crying. Melvin hasn't cried in years, not even when he and Rosie got divorced. Rosie, who's long since remarried and living with her husband in Tahoe, her other children right around the corner from them. No nursing home for her.

It's like this for a while, and then Mary blows her nose into a tissue. "I have to check on the others," she says. She gives him a hug and then slips away.

Melvin looks at the present on his nightstand. If he could have anything, what would it be? A new alarm clock maybe, but it seems inconsequential in light of what's happened. Alice fixed up and healthy once again? Even Melvin knows how ridiculous that request is.

He tugs at the corner of the paper. He can't tell what it

is, so he tears the paper a little more until the wrapping pulls away.

It's a box of Tifore's Lemon Creams. He stares at it in disbelief, at the gold stamped lettering, the cheery lemon printed on the cover of the box. These are the lemon creams of his childhood, a gift from his father's mother every Christmas season in preparation for the new year.

"The bitter with the sweet," she'd say, popping one in her mouth. She'd close her eyes and smile, a light dusting of powdered sugar still on her lips. Melvin would do the same, closing his eyes with a sense of contentment as the soft confection melted in his mouth.

Now, Melvin cracks the cellophane wrapping with a small pocketknife he keeps in the drawer by his bed. When he lifts the lid of the box, the room is filled with the scent of citrus and sugar. There are twelve yellow orbs, each tucked into their own square of the tray. He picks one up, feels the softness between his fingers, then puts it in his mouth.

The bitter with the sweet. The death of his younger brother at age five, a fall from an apple tree. Fighting with Rosie, the divorce. The death of his parents. The feeling of rejection when Barbara put him in Harmony Homes.

His first love at eleven, Juliet Rhodes. His first kiss. College, he was the first in his family to go. His first job, his marriage, his children. His grandmother. Lemon creams. Melvin closes his eyes, and remembers.

He's not sure why he gets up and walks to the hallway, makes his way to Alice Edwidge's room. Her room is a mess, a bit disheveled like Alice, her battered walker tossed in the corner, forlorn. *Charlie,* Melvin thinks with disdain. *Lifesaver, huh? You sure didn't do her any favors this morning.*

Melvin walks to the bed, the sheets still crumpled and unmade. Alice has hospital bars on the sides of her bed, which make it a bit difficult, but not impossible.

Melvin sets to work, starting at the bottom of the bed. He pulls the bottom sheet tight, tucking the end of the sheet between the mattress and the box spring. He moves to the head of the bed, and pulls the sheet taut, tucking that in, too.

Next he returns to the foot of the bed. He lifts the sheeting sixteen inches from the foot of the bed and places one finger on the top corner, lifting the sheet with his other hand. He tucks the lower drape under the mattress. Holding the corner in place, he brings the sheet over to form a forty-five degree angle. He tucks the rest of the side of the sheet under the mattress, working his way back to the top of the bed, smoothing as he goes. He does the same with the top sheet and then the blanket, then folds the comforter in thirds and places it at the foot of her bed.

It's funny, because Melvin makes his own bed twice a day, once in the morning and again after his nap. There's always a small pleasure in it, the contentment that comes with a job well done, but this feels so much more satisfying. He takes one last look, smooths a small winkle, and leaves.

On the way back to his room, he thinks about calling Barbara but then feels a part of him bristle. *Well, why not?* he argues with himself. Ask her if she'll come visit, or if he can stay with her a little longer. Promise not to cause any trouble, not to criticize her cooking. Volunteer to watch those grandkids of his, will try not to tell her how best to raise them. He'll just be there, trying not to cringe as he watches them tear open a million gifts too many, Barbara's way of making up for her lackluster ex-husband.

Melvin sighs, letting his shoulders drop. Maybe this is better, him being here. Barbara can have room to live her own life, make her own mistakes, without Melvin sitting on the sidelines shouting out what she should or shouldn't be doing. He's had a chance to live his life, and maybe now he has to give her a chance to live hers, too.

He passes Ella Steiner's room, sees the discards of her present in the large trashcan in the hallway. Inside, she's murmuring softly as she sets up a silver menorah in the window of her room. Funny how he never paid attention to her smile before or the way her silvery hair curls around her ear. He notices her hands, graceful, her fingers long and slender, and remembers that someone said she used to play the piano. He watches as she uses the center candle to light the first candle on the far left of the menorah. She looks up and gives him a shy smile.

Melvin feels heat rush to his cheeks. He gives her a polite nod and hurries on.

He passes Clark Peterson's room. "Melvin!" Clark calls, waving a miniature cue in the air. "Did you hear about Alice Edwidge?"

"I was there, Mr. Peterson," Melvin says. "We all were. It's very sad."

"No, Melvin, the latest news. She's going to be all right! Damn walker broke her fall, she has a concussion and a fractured wrist, but she's fine. They might be sending her home as soon as tomorrow or the day after."

Home. Is this what that is?

"Hey, wanna play some snooker?" Clark asks. "I have two cues!"

Melvin's about to decline when he thinks, why not? "Sure," he steps, stepping into Clark's room. It's the first time he's ever been inside. It's cleaner than he expected. The TV is the most prominent feature in the room, next to the bed that Clark spends his days in.

They play four rounds before Melvin calls it quits. "Long day," he says. "Thanks for the game."

"Re-match tomorrow?"

Melvin grins. "Sure."

Back in his room, Melvin readies for bed. He changes

his clothes and brushes his teeth, turns out the light. He slips in between his sheets, lets out a deep breath. His room still smells of lemon creams, and he's decided he's going to save the rest to share with the others. Mary, of course, and Alice when she returns. Ella, if she eats sweets, and Clark, whom Melvin suspects eats nothing but sugar when he's camped out in front of the TV. Maybe he'll send a box to Barbara and the kids.

He drifts into a dreamless sleep, a smile on his lips.

Outside the Pick and Save

THE LINE STARTED AT THE ENTRANCE of the Pick and Save and wrapped around the block, forty people long.

It's early still, just past seven, but people have been standing in line for almost an hour. Most people are bundled up warm and a few people have brought blankets from their cars and trucks.

"A free Christmas turkey!" Enid Griffin declares. She's thirteenth in line. "Honestly, I'm surprised more people aren't here." She looks around, stamping her feet to keep warm.

"Is there a limit?" Jannell Mason asks anxiously.

"One per family," Goldie Little tells her. She heard about the giveaway less than twenty-four hours ago from Erwin Holder, a clerk at the Pick and Save who came in for his twice annual haircut at the Avalon Cut and Curl.

Jannell counts the number of people in line. "What if they run out?" she asks.

At this thought a few panicked faces turn toward the locked doors of the Pick and Save. They still have ten minutes to go. Harriet Simpson has a strategy to make sure she gets her turkey of choice. Once inside the Pick and Save, she'll make a sharp right towards the produce department and then follow the heads of lettuce and tomatoes straight to the meats in the back of the store. She considered cutting through the aisles in a diagonal pattern but is worried others might do the same, causing a jam in the pasta and juice aisles and thus slowing her down. No, better to follow the widest path and proceed in a straight line.

Merv Stanton was getting gas when he saw people lining up. He figured something interesting was going on so he decided to check it out. He waited in line for almost ten minutes before asking someone what they were doing there.

"I've already made plans for my free holiday turkey," Corey Baker tells the woman standing next to him. He's in his mid-twenties, a subcontractor with a local construction company in town. "I've invited two friends over from work. I'll be doing baked potatoes and green beans."

"I have a recipe for scalloped potatoes that's easy," Felicity Banks tells him. "You can make it in just five steps. If you have paper I'm happy to give you the recipe now."

"Sure, why not?" Corey nods in thanks as a man in front of him hands him a section of his paper and a pen.

"Four potatoes, one medium onion, four tablespoons flour," Felicity recites, ticking off each ingredient on her fingertips as Corey begins to write. "Four tablespoons butter, salt and pepper to taste..."

"Oh, there is nothing finer than a turkey coming out of the oven," Enid sighs. "Every year I soak mine in brine. Meat just falls off the bones!"

"What's brine?" Ishmael Pope asks. He's not in line for a turkey, just hoping to get dibs on the fresh produce that's brought in every Friday morning. He likes to shop early so he's usually here when the doors open. He can be in and out in less than ten minutes with over two recyclable bags filled with his groceries for the week. The unexpected crowd of people is both annoying but a bit intriguing, too. A loner, Ishmael hasn't been around this many people in a long time.

"Brine is a salt water soak," Enid tells him. "It makes everything more tender and so much more tastier. I brine everything."

"My grandmother used to make her own pickles," Ishmael recalls. "I think that's how she did it. It would take forever before those pickles were ready." He remembers dusty jars lining the wooden shelves in the cellar.

"If it was four to six weeks, then she probably used a brine solution," Enid says. "You can pickle faster with vinegar, but it's still a good week or two if you want the flavor."

"Enid, that pickled slaw you brought to the Fourth of July picnic this past year was delicious with the burgers and steaks," someone says, sighing at the memory.

"Oh, that one's easy," Enid says. "Red cabbage, onions, sugar, salt and pepper, and you're done! Oh, and the vinegar, of course." She laughs.

"Here," Corey says, tearing off a strip of newspaper and handing the rest to Ishmael along with the pen. "If you want to take notes."

Ishmael listens to Enid repeat the ingredients, asking a question or two then taking down her number at Avalon Travel in case he has any more questions.

"Dessert is always my problem," Noelle "Noe" Hart says. She's not from Avalon, but here because an aunt just died. For the past six days Noe has been rambling about her aunt's large weathered house, piles of things everywhere, feeling overwhelmed and alone. It was the real estate agent who suggested Noe take a break and just enjoy Avalon for a couple of days. She gave Noe a list of things to do, including standing outside the Pick and Save for her free turkey.

"Dessert is our favorite part!" Priya Blair declares. Her

identical twin sister, Lori, nods in agreement. The only distinguishing features between the two young women is that Priya has a pink scarf wrapped around her leather jacket while Lori has a light blue one. They're in their early twenties and standing a few people behind Noe, but listening to everything that's going on. "Next to chili, that is."

"And buffalo wings," Lori adds, smacking her lips.

"Agreed," Priya says. She gives Noe a smile. "Anyway, you have to ask yourself a central question first. What do you prefer, sweet or savory?"

Noe thinks. The first thing that comes to mind, more of a smell really, is her mother's apple pie. "Sweet," she says. "Definitely sweet."

"Oh, I love your accent," Lori says. "You're not from here, are you?"

"Texas," Noe says, blushing. This is the first time she's left the south, much less the state of Texas, so she knows she stands out with her light southern drawl.

Priya smiles. "Well, welcome to Avalon. So you like sweet things. Are you a chocolate person?"

Noe laughs, feels a tightness that's been in her chest all week start to loosen. "Isn't everyone?"

"Not me," Enid says. "I'm very particular about where I get my calories. Chocolate isn't one of them."

"Not even hot chocolate?" Harriet asks in surprise as Enid shakes her head. "What about white chocolate?"

"White chocolate really isn't chocolate," Milly Walton tells them from the front of the line. "It's cocoa butter and milk solids."

Priya looks at Noe. "What about cookies or cakes?" she asks. "Or are you more of pudding person?"

"Cookies," Noe says.

The sisters look at each other before breaking out into a

grin. "Then we have the perfect recipe for you," Priya says. "It's easy and full of chocolate. Chocolate crackle cookies!"

There's a murmur of agreement as the women surrounding the twins and Noe nod.

"Okay, let me write this down," Noe says. She looks through her purse for something to write with when someone nudges her and passes her a pen and the remaining sheet of newspaper. "Okay, go ahead."

"One cup Amish Friendship Bread starter," Priya begins. "Half cup brown sugar, packed…"

Dale Hodge, manager for the Pick and Save, unlocks one of the doors and steps outside. The crowd hushes and Noe lowers her pen, feels a rush of adrenaline.

"Okay, folks," he says. "A few ground rules: no running, no pushing. There are plenty of turkeys, more than those of you standing in line, so you'll all get one. And I just received word that the same anonymous benefactor is giving away the hams, too. So it's your choice: ham or turkey, but you can only choose one. And only one free turkey or ham per household, please."

There's a small commotion as some people are thrown into indecision.

"Burl loves ham!" someone cries to her friend. "But I was going to do a turkey! I have the menu all planned out!"

"My wife makes it with this brown sugar pineapple glaze," one man tells another, blowing on his hands. "Grandkids love it. But I'm a turkey man myself. Darned if I know what to do now."

"Who's giving this away again?" Goldie asks, but no one seems to hear her.

"I was going to buy a ham anyway," Jannell says, beaming. "Now I can buy a turkey or ham *and* get the other for free." A look of anxiety crosses her face. "But which one should I buy and which one should I get for free?"

"Just buy whichever's cheaper," someone says impatiently, craning their neck as they watch Dale Hodge unlock the other side of the door.

"No, you need to figure out how many servings you'll get," Emmett Jensen says. He's an accountant, buried under three scarves and woolly earmuffs. The minute Dale made the announcement, he decided to go with a honey-baked ham for his holiday table, which seems more traditional than turkey. He'll be cooking for his new girlfriend and her son, and he already did a turkey for Thanksgiving. "Look at the cost per pound although the turkey has more bone, so you have to discount that. For example, a fifteen-pound turkey that serves six versus a ham that serves …"

"Oh, for goodness sake!" Carol Doyle snaps. "It's just Christmas dinner, not rocket science!"

"Yeah," her friend, Jo Kay Buckley, retorts. They're young mothers in their mid-thirties, both with four children apiece. They're wearing workout clothes under their puffy down jackets, their children still at home with their husbands who will shuttle them to all the appropriate places: school or daycare, the babies with a shared sitter. The women are irritable until they have their morning coffee which can't happen until after their "me" time which is a workout at the gym in Freeport with a personal trainer named Stanton.

"It's not rocket science," Emmett agrees, unperturbed. He could never date women like Carol or Jo Kay, both of whom he knows from high school. They didn't care for him then and it's clear they don't care for him now, but that doesn't bother him. He knows he's a geek while they were two of the most popular girls in school, but they're not in high school anymore. Emmett has his own accounting firm, makes a good living, and is dating a nice woman named Janice. "It's just simple math, Jokey." He grins.

Jo Kay glares at him.

Dale Hodge finishes unlocking the doors and steps to the side, his ring of keys jingling. "Come on in, everyone! Remember, no pushing!"

There's a small surge as people press forward, chattering excitedly. In a matter of minutes the store is full of people, and more keep coming.

"This is going to be crazy," Rhea Higbee, a cashier, tells another cashier, Cassie Gaines. No one is checking out yet, but they're ready.

"I know," Cassie says. She takes one last chew of gum before tossing it in the trash. "Remember the time we double downed for the week?"

Rhea grins. In an effort to make the Pick and Save a coupon-friendly grocery store, the management had decided to let customers double the value of their manufacturer coupons with a limit of ten coupons per day. Customers had gone nuts and the week was exhausting, but it had been fun.

Cassie nods as the first wave of customers holding their turkeys or ham approach the registers. "Here we go!" she says. She fastens on a smile, her hands ready to scan the first item.

On Aisle Six—Pasta, Rice, Dried Beans, and Pudding Snacks—Wanda Sharpe stands in front of a shelf full of instant stuffing. She points to a box.

"Now I know from experience that this cornbread stuffing has excellent taste and texture," she's telling Edie Gallagher, who's taking copious notes. "But it can run a little dry, so I tend to be generous with the butter. If you love cornbread, this is the stuffing for you."

Edie nods. Her baby daughter, Miranda, is sitting in the cart along with Edie's own turkey, patting it like it's a cat. Edie is a reporter with the *Avalon Gazette* and they're running a story on the free turkey and ham giveaway. Edie plans to put a few recipes in with the article, but she wants to find out who's behind the giveaway. So far no one has stepped forward and Dale Hodges says he doesn't know either, just that someone dropped off a cashier's check with instructions that they make a ham or turkey available to every family in Avalon who wants one. There's over four thousand people in Avalon, about fifteen hundred households. Edie knows not everyone will come by, but still. That's a lot of free meat even for someone imbued with Christmas spirit. They'd have to have pretty deep pockets, too.

"Now, if you know you're going to have turkey on the table, you'll want to go with this." Wanda points to another box. "The right balance of spices and herbs, not too salty. You can even see bits of celery and onion, though I always chop up a little extra on my own and add it as well. It's just like homemade!"

"Except that it's not," Agnes Reyes sniffs from behind them. Her own cart is filled with onions and celery, a bag of walnuts, currants, green apples and, of course, a turkey. "The holidays are a time for friends and family to come together. Who wants stuffing out of a box?"

"I do," Wanda informs her. "As you said, the holidays are about spending time with the people you love. Who wants to be slaving away in a kitchen all day? Not me, that's who."

Agnes reaches past them for a bag of brown rice. "I make a turkey and rice soup the day after," she tells Edie. "I'd be happy to give you that or the stuffing recipe for the *Gazette*. Real recipes, not with instructions that say 'add hot water and mix thoroughly.'" She gives Wanda a haughty look.

"The good citizens of Avalon want quick and easy tips," Wanda tells Edie firmly, stepping in front of Agnes. She reaches over and clucks as she tickles Miranda's cheeks.

"You want to be able to enjoy these moments. Goodness knows you're busy enough as a new mom. Do you really have time to toast walnuts or make your own stock?"

"Graham loves my turkey stuffing—the stock is what gives it the flavor," Agnes retorts. She turns to Edie. "Don't you have a favorite recipe from your childhood? Food is how people show love for one another. You're preparing something from your heart. When your daughter grows up, she won't remember what you got her for all those birthdays, all those toys and other nonsense. What she'll remember is what you put on the table. The smells of her childhood." Agnes straightens up. "If you'd like, I'm happy to be interviewed to discuss this in greater detail. I'm free on Friday."

Wanda puts her hands on her hips, annoyed. "Agnes, Edie is interviewing *me*. ME. You've had your time in the sun, it's my turn now." She turns to Edie. "Agnes used to have a column in the *Gazette*, like thirty years ago. Op Ed." She rolls her eyes.

"It was called 'Agnes' Angle,'" Agnes tells Edie, her face lighting up. "Predated you and that editor of yours. My column ran for five years. Avalonians loved it—I've kept all of my fan mail."

Wanda is just staring at the ceiling, annoyed.

Miranda is starting to get fussy, and Edie needs to get home, needs to start typing up her notes if she wants to meet her deadline. "Why don't I get both of your numbers?" she suggests. "That way I can call if I have any questions. As you both know, we have limited space in the *Gazette*, so I won't be able to use both recipes."

Agnes hands Edie a strip of newspaper. "Well, I already took the liberty of jotting down the recipe for you, just in case. Here you go!"

"Agnes Reyes, you were eavesdropping!" Wanda

exclaims. "You've been trying to finagle your way into this conversation ever since we started at the jellied cranberries—I thought that was you behind the display of canned green beans. I'll bet you don't even need that brown rice!"

Agnes looks defensive, and then guilty. "It's true, I don't." She puts the one-pound bag back on the shelf and explains to Edie, "I can get it for a dollar twenty-five when it's on sale—I almost never pay regular price if I can help it. Hey, do you suppose your readers might appreciate some shopping tips as well?"

"NO," Wanda says before Edie can answer. She crosses her arms and gives Agnes a pointed look.

"Well, there's no need to get worked up, Wanda," Agnes says, lifting her chin. "I have to go now anyways. Graham will be up soon and I have to make him breakfast."

Wanda looks startled. "What do you mean?" she asks.

"Graham, my husband? He was sleeping when I left." Agnes hums as she checks her shopping list against the items in her cart. "Wanda, I know you think it's nonsense but I'm telling you—my food has only made my marriage better. Fifty years and counting." She puts her hands on the handle of her cart and Edie can see that her wedding band and diamond ring are still sparkling. "Well, I'll be going. Happy holidays, all."

Wanda touches Agnes on the arm, turns to Edie. Her voice is low. "You know, on second thought, I think you should put Agnes' stuffing recipe in the *Gazette*. She's right—people don't need instructions on how to make instant stuffing. I mean, it's right there on the package, after all."

Edie's confused. "Okay, but…"

"Agnes, let me walk you home," Wanda says. She begins pushing her cart alongside Agnes who's already heading down the aisle. "Now how far in advance should I make that stuffing…"

Edie watches, bewildered, until someone comes up next to her.

"Mr. Reyes died three years ago," a young man says. His name is Caleb Vinson, and he lives right down the street from the Reyes. He used to mow their lawn every other Saturday, help shovel snow from the driveway every winter. Of course, that was a long time ago and he's a recent college grad, back in Avalon for the holidays. The whole Vinson clan is here and he's the only Vinson not in a committed relationship. He keeps telling his parents that he just hasn't met the right girl, that he's not in any sort of rush. That doesn't stop them from trying to set him up with every available coed in Avalon, which is weird because he knows almost everyone. "Mrs. Reyes forgets sometimes."

"That's so sad," Edie says. She reaches down and lifts Miranda out of the cart. She holds her close and her daughter softens against her, nestling her head in the crook of Edie's neck. Edie breathes in daughter's sweet scent and thinks about her own husband, Richard, the town's GP.

"Most days Mrs. Reyes knows, and she's good with it. She just misses him." Caleb is holding two boxes of vanilla instant pudding, his cart filled with tell-tale ingredients for Amish Friendship Bread—cinnamon and sugar, vanilla, flour and eggs. "My grandmother is here from St. Louis so I stole my mom's recipe for Amish Friendship Bread. I'm going to try the stollen variation. I didn't know you could make so many different things from that basic recipe."

"I personally know of more than two hundred and fifty," Edie says with a shake of her head. The only problem with being a reporter is the tendency to keep every last detail in your head. Last year when the town baked Amish Friendship Bread Edie had gained serious weight, in part because she was eating the bread and in part because she found out she was pregnant. "Breads and cakes, cookies, pancakes, you name it. But I am Amish Friendship Breaded out."

"My grandmother's made it for years," Caleb tells her. "She'd send it to me at school, which was cool." He pulls a piece of paper out of his back pocket and frowns. "But it looks like the Pick and Save doesn't have any marzipan."

"Almonds, sugar and water," a young woman says as she passes by. "I'm heading over to Nuts and Dried Fruit as we speak. I can show you."

Caleb smiles. "Thank you." He gives Edie a wave and follows the woman towards Aisle Four.

"Let's see," the young woman says. Her fingers skim the shelves and Caleb sees she has dried paint on her fingers, a pretty forest green. She plucks a bag of almonds off the shelf and hands it to him. "It's better with the skin on," she tells him. "It tastes fresher that way."

"Okay…" Caleb doesn't look convinced. He weighs the bag in his hand.

The woman laughs. "Marzipan is an almond paste," she says. "So all you have to do is boil the almonds, peel them, then grind them up. Add sugar and water and you're done."

He sighs. "I think I'm in over my head. Maybe I should just stick with the basic recipe."

"What are you making?"

"Friendship bread. It's kind of a family tradition. My grandmother used to make a stollen every Christmas and I thought I'd make it for her this year."

"That's nice. Traditions are a good thing to have. And I think you should give it a try—even if it doesn't turn out right, you gave it a go, right?"

That sounds just like something his grandmother would say. Caleb tosses the almonds into his cart. "Okay. Sold."

The young woman smiles and holds out a paint-stained hand. "Emily Cochran."

"Caleb Vinson." They shake hands and Caleb feels like the light in the store has suddenly become brighter.

"Oh, gosh, sorry about that." Emily flips her palms over and Caleb sees a rainbow of colors, warm yellows and oranges, bright pinks and blues. "I was up all night working on a commission. It's dry, don't worry."

Caleb just grins. "I wasn't worried."

Emily blushes and peers into his cart. "You already have the powdered sugar, so it looks like you're set. You can get the recipe off the internet or…" She fumbles through her purse and hands him a business card. "Or stop by the gallery. Well, I call it a gallery but it's more of a working art studio. And by working art studio, I mean the loft where I live." She gives him a sheepish smile.

Caleb looks at the card. EMILY COCHRAN. ARTIST. There's an address and a phone number.

"Oh wait, that number's old," Emily says. She looks for a pen as she says, embarrassed, "I keep losing my cell phone. I don't even know where it is half the time." She keeps burrowing through her purse. "Shoot, I thought I had a pen."

"Here," Noe says. She's standing next to them, going through the shopping list for the chocolate crackle cookies. She hefts a bag of brown sugar and a tin of baking soda into her cart. She offers a pen to Emily with a smile.

"Gee, thanks," Emily says. She crosses out the phone number on her business card and writes in the new one and hands it back to Caleb. Her fingertips brush his arm and that's all it takes for him to know that he wants to see her again. He watches as she tucks a stray strand of hair behind her ear and smiles the most beautiful smile he's ever seen.

"You have a gallery?" Noe asks, interested.

Emily nods, fishes another card out of her purse. She studies Noe with interest. "Artist?" she asks.

Noe's cheeks flush red. "I do some illustrations," she says, "But it's more for fun. I don't think I could make a living from it." She looks at Emily's card, wistful.

"That's what I used to say," Emily tells her. "Come by the studio some time. We'll talk." She turns to Caleb. "And you'll call? I mean, if you need any help?" Her cheeks pink.

He grins. "I'll definitely need help and I'm definitely calling."

"Okay. Bye." Emily smiles at Noe and Caleb as she pushes her way towards the cash registers.

Emily's exhausted, that's true, and ready to hit the sack as soon as she gets home and gets this turkey in the fridge. But she feels a nervous excitement, sort of like the first time she sold a painting.

As the cashier rings her up, Emily clicks the pen as she thinks about what just happened. She doesn't get out much, and even when she does, she's not much for socializing. She just doesn't have time for it, her work is always calling her and if she's not working, she's catching up on sleep. But already she's met two new people, too close to her age to be able to afford her artwork, but people she already likes whom she can see becoming friends. Emily's always trusted her instincts, and she knows that Caleb could be more. She can't wait to find out.

"Ten dollars and seventeen cents," Rhea tells her. "You picked a good turkey. A big one."

"It's twenty pounds. I'll be eating turkey for a year." Emily brings out her checkbook, hands Rhea her ID. "Not that I'm complaining. I love turkey. It was nice, whoever did this."

"Yeah, there are rumors but no one knows who's giving them away. It's good business for the Pick and Save, so we're not complaining." Rhea tucks the receipt into the bag. "Bettie Shelton and the ladies of the Avalon Scrapbooking Society made a large card for the person who donated all the turkeys. Since we don't know who that is, we're just leaving it there, at the front of the store." Rhea points. "You can sign the card if you want."

"Yes, absolutely," Emily says, picking up her bags. "Thanks, Rhea."

"Merry Christmas, Emily."

Emily walks to the front of the store where a large piece of cardstock is decorated with a live wreath, small paper presents, bells, and other holiday embellishments tucked into the greenery. A red velvet bow graces the top of the wreath. THANK YOU GENEROUS BENEFACTOR, reads the card.

Emily takes the pen from her purse and signs the card.

Gift Wrapped

⌒∕∕⌒

MARGOT WEST IS WALKING to the gift shop she owns on Fifth and Main. It's a cold, brisk morning and she's walking fast, anxious to get to the store even though she has more than an hour before opening time.

She wants to turn on the lights for the Christmas village display in the window, open the day's door on her advent calendar, turn on the CD player with a selection of her favorite Christmas carols. She'll roll the oversized wooden nutcracker onto the sidewalk, put out the chalkboard sign with a red and white striped pole that says SANTA'S WORKSHOP THIS WAY with an arrow pointing into the shop. Inside she has free mini candy canes for the kids, mulled apple cider for the adults, and everyone who spends more than ten dollars in her shop gets free gift wrap and a chance to win one of her fabulous bath and body baskets.

Christmas is Margot's favorite holiday of the year. Easter is a close second, as is Valentine's Day, but there's something about the magic of the season that makes her heart stir. It's the anticipation, she decides. The wrapped presents under the tree, the waiting, the expectation. The giving as well as the receiving. Everybody wins.

"Oh, you're like any other retailer around the holidays,"

her partner Gordon will tease. "It's just another chance to make loads of money." She'll deny it, but it's true, because shopping is part of what makes Christmas so fun. The festive decorations, the smells, the sounds. Finding that right gift. Choosing the right paper. Placing it under the tree. Margot already has Gordon's gift—he's a bit of a garden buff, and wintertime is hard on him because he can't be outside tending to his plants. She found a fancy high-tech planter that will let Gordon plant herbs, salad greens and tomatoes and grow them indoors. She's keeping it hidden in the store with all her inventory so he doesn't get a whiff of what she bought him, at least not yet. He'll sometimes complain that she gives him too many gifts, and Margot will tell him that gift giving is part of who she is. She opened the store with that express purpose in mind, after all.

She and Gordon aren't married, Gordon having divorced his first wife almost twenty years ago and Margot just never having found the right person. Boyfriend and girlfriend sounds too juvenile for people in their sixties. They've been together eight years, share a home, and for all intents and purposes are as committed a couple as any couple could be. And yet…well, there's no point in going there anymore. They've had the discussion so many times and once it almost ended things altogether. Gordon isn't a proponent of marriage and Margot wishes his first wife hadn't spoiled it for him. It could be different, or so she thinks, but it just makes Gordon shut down whenever she brings it up. So for the past three years she hasn't, and she doesn't intend to again.

Margot walks on. Already her sales for the month are exceeding her expectations, and she expects it to get better as last-minute shoppers scramble for the perfect gift. Grandparents will be coming in to town to celebrate with their children and grandchildren, and Margot's made sure her toy selection is well stocked. There are also husbands, frantic for the perfect gift, running into her store without a clue as to what their wives might want or need. Margot tries not to judge and besides, that's why she's here. To help people find that perfect gift.

She stops when she turns the corner. There, in front of her store, is a man setting up a metal card table. A cardboard box filled with rolls of wrapping paper rests on the rustic wooden bench she's placed outside for customers to sit on. Next to the box is a droopy poinsettia in a cracked plastic container. When she sees him put up his sign, she sets her mouth and marches over.

"Excuse me!" she says.

The man looks up. "Yes?" he says.

"I'm Margot West, owner of Avalon Gifts 'N More. I'm afraid you can't set up right in front of my store." She gives a polite but firm smile.

The man looks around. "I thought the sidewalk was common use," he says.

"Well, yes. For merchants who pay rent."

The man shakes his head. "I don't think so." He jiggles the table, pulls a small square of cardboard from his pocket and slips it under one of the table legs. "Sidewalks are public domain, ma'am."

Margot stiffens. She doesn't like the look of this fellow. He's in his late forties with dark hair and brooding eyes, and it doesn't look like he hasn't shaved this morning or even the day before. Margot's lived in Avalon almost all her life and while it's true there's been an influx of new residents, she doesn't recognize him at all.

"For walking," Margot says. "Pedestrian traffic. Not for…this." She gestures to his sign.

The man looks at the sign as if seeing it for the first time. "I think it'll be all right," he says with a shrug. He lays out a few supplies on his table—scissors, tape, a basket of bows and a large spool of red ribbon. Then he attaches his sign to the front of his table.

FREE GIFT WRAPPING SERVICE

Margot frowns. She's offering free gift wrap in the store, so it's not as if he's stealing any business from her. Still, she doesn't like it. She works hard to create a warm and inviting storefront and walkway, and the exterior is just as important to her as the interior of the store. This ramshackle operation just won't do. She has rights here, too.

"I'm sorry," Margot says, "but I'm going to have to ask you to leave. Or set up your table down there, somewhere." She makes a vague gesture down the street. "What about near the pharmacy?"

The man opens a rusty folding chair and sits down, lacing his fingers together and resting them on the table. "Nope. I'm good, thanks."

Margot just shakes her head as she unlocks the front door and flicks on the lights. She could call the police, she supposes, but she doesn't want that kind of trouble. Maybe he'll be here for a couple of hours and that will be that.

She inhales deeply, the scent of peppermint tickling her nose. She feels herself calm as she goes to the back room and shrugs off her coat and scarf, tucking her gloves into her purse. The store is her sanctuary, filled with items she loves. She presses PLAY on the CD player and the melodious strains of "White Christmas" waft through the store. A second later, she's humming along.

Oh, she hopes it'll start snowing soon. They had an early snowfall in November and there's always a smattering of snowflakes here and there but so far nothing has stuck on the ground for very long. Margot loves that first heavy snowfall, the kind that makes everyone homebound, schools and businesses closed for the day, the streets piled high with white fluffy snow. Of course that's only in the beginning— once the snow turns black and icy, it becomes more of an annoyance but still Margot can't imagine going through winter without a white Christmas. How people can live in Florida or Hawaii she'll never understand.

She starts to open the boxes that were delivered the day before, gasping in delight with each one. Some new bottlecap jewelry from Ava Catalina, a local artist, and a wonderful collection of purses and pillows made from old potato burlap bags and vintage fabrics from a farm just outside of Avalon. She's already sold out of Maureen Nyer's holiday crocheted afghans but Maureen just dropped off several scarves and wraps that Margot knows she can sell in a heartbeat as soon as she sets them out. There's also a selection of new candle pillars from Lessie Matthews, a woman who's been supplying Margot with fragrant hand-poured soaps and candles ever since she opened the shop.

The next hour flies by with Margot putting out new items and rearranging displays. She makes a few phone calls and pays a few bills, and when it's ten o'clock, Margot turns the sign from CLOSED to OPEN.

Through the glass she sees the man sitting at his table, his hands still folded in front of him. There's a weathered paperback face down on the table. Margot can't see the title, but it doesn't matter. He's not doing much of a sales job, Margot thinks as she walks back to the register.

There's a small gust of wind as the door is pushed open and Shari Hewitt walks in. Shari is a young mom who sent her only child off to kindergarten this past fall and is still trying to figure out how to spend her days. She comes to the store at least once a week looking at new items or buying gifts for family and friends.

"Morning, Shari," Margot says. "Could I offer you some mulled cider?"

"Good morning, Margot," Shari says, giving a shiver. "Mulled cider sounds wonderful. Temperature's been dropping all week—I keep having to change our thermostat or we just can't warm up." She looks around the store. "Anything new today?"

"Lots. And I got more of those rainbow nesting mixing bowls that you've been admiring," Margot tells her. She pours Shari a cup of cider and hands it to her. "Don't forget I'm offering free gift wrap whenever you spend ten dollars or more, even if you're buying a gift for yourself!"

Shari laughs as she blows on the cider before taking a sip. "Matt has been asking me what I want for Christmas. I keep thinking I should ask for something glamorous but all I really want are kitchen items. Maybe I should just buy it and let Matt put it under the tree for me."

"Well, let me know," Margot says. "I have three in stock and I'm not planning to order more until the spring."

Shari nods, lingering by the fuzzy slippers. "So did you see the guy outside? The one with the gift wrap station?"

Margot glances out the window. "Oh, him. Yes, I saw him when I opened up this morning. Did he give you any trouble?" She feels herself bristle.

"Oh no," Shari sighs, running her fingers over a wind chime. "He was actually quite polite. It's so clever, don't you think? And such a good service, too. I wonder how he can do it for free—I bet a lot of people will go to him. I mean, even I'm terrible when it comes to wrapping things. Layla does a better job than me!" Layla is Shari's five-year old daughter.

Margot pretends to straighten out a rack of bejeweled reading glasses. "Well, you don't know what kind of a job he'll do either," she says. "My experience is that you get what you pay for. And his paper selection seems a little plain. I mean, if that matters to you."

Shari offers her an awkward smile. "It just seems like a good idea, with everyone so busy during the holidays."

Taking advantage is more like it, Margot thinks, because she's sure he's got an ulterior motive. Margot prides herself on being able to read people and he's hiding something, she can tell. Instead she says, "Take your time looking around, Shari, and let me know if you'd like any more of that cider." The door opens and another customer walks in.

"Welcome to Avalon Gifts 'N More!" Margot calls out, grateful for the interruption. "Might I interest you in a cup of warm mulled cider while you shop?"

The rest of the morning unfolds with customers coming and going. Margot keeps busy answering questions and ringing up purchases. At one point there's a line ten people deep.

She should have hired extra help for the holidays. That's one of the disadvantages to only being in business a year— she's still working out the kinks.

"Just a moment!" she calls out to a woman who's asking questions about a trio of apothecary jars.

"I can just take my items outside to get wrapped," Hazel Thomas tells her as Margot rings her up. "I don't mind." She has a scarf, two glass vases, and a leather jewelry box. Hazel's married to the town pharmacist, Clyde, and Margot plays Bunco with her every other Thursday night. Margot knows Hazel's just trying to help out with her suggestion but it causes a stir as everyone's head swivels towards the sidewalk.

"I forgot about that," someone says, nodding. "That would speed things up. I heard that a few people tried to give him a donation and he wouldn't accept it. He insisted that it was free."

"No minimum purchase, eh?" someone chuckles from the back. It's Evelyn Underwood, that witch.

"I have a few jams and jellies I picked up at the farmer's market this morning," Irma Fagen says. She's the owner at the Avalon Gutter, the town's bowling alley. "He could just wrap everything for me. Would sure save me the trouble." She looks at her watch. "I have to get going soon—gotta open up the lanes for the Early Birds. It's a new senior bowling league," she explains to Octavia Stout, who's standing in line behind her. Octavia's arms are full candles, soaps, and a large stuffed teddy bear.

Someone else sighs as they check their watch. "I have to drive into Barrett for a lunch date. I'm going to be late."

"I'm not in a rush, you can go ahead of me," the person in front of her offers.

Margot listens to the women talking, feels her own stress level beginning to rise.

"If you'd like, I can ring people up now and you can get on your way," she says to everyone. She forces a bright smile. "Then you can pick up your gifts at a time that's more convenient for you."

A couple heads nod but there are a few doubtful looks as well. It's only a Band-Aid to a bigger problem, which is that Margot can't take care of her customers at the moment.

"You know, I think I will just take these outside," Hazel says as Margot hands her the receipt.

"Oh. Well, all right," Margot says. She bags up Hazel's gifts. "I can also include some gift wrap paper and ribbon in the bag if you'd like to wrap it at home."

"Thanks, Margot, but I'll pass. If I can help it I won't have to worry about wrapping a single present this year." Hazel gives her a wave as she heads out the door.

"I don't need mine gift wrapped either," the next person tells Margot.

"Me neither."

"Nor me."

Only one person—Ramona Garza, wife of their local fire chief—seems interested in having Margot wrap her presents.

Well, that's fine. It was a complimentary service anyway, but Margot feels bad that she's not offering the full service that she promised. She finishes ringing up all the customers in line and wrapping Ramona's presents, then drops onto the wooden stool by the register, exhausted.

"Just this," Shari says, stepping up to the register. She's been in the shop for most of the morning, lingering here and there, and Margot had almost forgotten she was there. Shari places a small decorative pillow embroidered with purple violets, Illinois' state flower.

"What about those nesting bowls?" Margot asks. She already sold one this morning, which means there are only two left.

Shari blushes. "I do love them," she admits. "But they're a little pricey and the truth is, we're on a budget. I've been doing a bit too much retail therapy these last few months. I'm still not used to being home without Layla." She gives a shy smile.

Margot tucks a few extra candy canes into the bag. "Well, I certainly appreciate all the business you've given me, Shari. I'll be having a big sale in the new year so I'll be sure to send you a postcard once I have that date set. Would you like me to wrap the pillow?"

"Yes, please." Shari's gaze drifts outside. "Wow, he sure is busy," she says. "Even if it is starting to snow."

Margot follows Shari's gaze and sure enough, fat flakes of snow are coming down in spirals. She sees a line has formed on the sidewalk, people bundled up and laughing, bags bulging with gifts waiting to be wrapped.

"Hmm," Margot says as she holds out a selection of gift bows. "Red, green or silver?"

"Silver." Shari looks back outside again. "Oh, look. It's really starting to come down."

Margot looks back outside. There's a veil of white as snow comes down thicker and heavier—beautiful, yes, but from the looks of it, this is the snowstorm Margot's been waiting for.

"It looks like he'll have his hands full for the rest of the day," Shari says.

"He'll have frostbite before this day is over," Margot says, her lips set tight. "Though I have a feeling we'll all be heading home early anyway." There's a chance they might be snowed in tomorrow, too. It's a good thing she had a busy morning.

The door opens, ushering in a flurry of snowflakes.

"Someone said you're giving away hot cider and cocoa," Travis Fields says. He's a young guy, and Margot recognizes him from the copy store. "It sure is nice and warm in here!"

"Feel free to look around," Margot tells him as she hands him a steaming cup of cocoa.

"Nah, I already got what I need." He nods to the bag in his hand. "Just waitin' outside to get them wrapped. Thanks for this!" He gives Margot a smile and is about to leave when he says, "Oh, could I get a cup of cider, too? For my girlfriend? She's holding our place in line."

Grrr. Margot tries to keep a pleasant smile on her face as she readies the cider. Well, now that he's been in the store maybe he'll be back. Future customer. It's a small investment, right?

Except that more people start coming in, not to shop but to warm up and get a free beverage. Margot tries not to panic as she notices how wet her floor is getting, and does a quick pass with the mop as people come in and out.

"Do you need any help?" Shari asks. She's standing by the small selection of artisan chocolates, her own purchase in hand, not in any hurry to get home.

"Goodness, Shari, you're still here?" Margot exclaims. "You should get home while you can."

"I just checked with the school and they're going to let the kids out at the regular time," says Shari. "So I have a couple more hours to myself. I can give you a hand, if you want. You wouldn't have to pay me, Margot. I admire how you're filled with so much Christmas spirit, letting people warm up inside even though they're not buying anything. And you're giving away all your cider and cocoa."

"Well, I'm almost out," Margot says, checking the carafes. "Just enough left for a cup or two." Without meaning to, she looks outside.

His line is longer than before, and Margot can see that the man behind the table is doing his best to wrap presents despite the turn in weather.

"I'll take you up on your offer," Margot says, reaching for her coat. She pours the last of the cider into one of the commuter thermoses she sells by the register. "Help me move these displays against the side of the wall and run the mop across the floor whenever it looks like it's getting wet. And if you want to work mornings for the rest of the month, I'd be grateful for the help."

"Oh yes!" Shari breathes. She puts her purchase behind the register and reaches for the mop.

"And I will pay you for your time," Margot continues as she grabs scissors and tape. "I didn't budget for any shop help, but I could do twelve dollars an hour. Plus you'll get an employee discount of thirty percent off anything in the store."

Shari beams. "Thirty percent? Really?"

Margot nods as she heads out the door. "Really."

She gives a shiver as she steps out of the warmth of her store. Already the pavement is covered with snow. There are grumbles as she pushes past people to reach the front of the line.

The man looks up, his woolen hat pulled below his ears, his nose bright red. Margot sees that his mittens have the fingers snipped off at the tips so he can handle the paper and tape with ease. She also sees that he's going to freeze to death if he doesn't get inside soon.

"Sorry to block the entrance to your store," the man says. "I didn't expect so many people."

Margot just shrugs. "It looks like you're doing quite well for yourself." She looks down the line. "And it looks like you're making quite a few people happy, too. Everyone seems to be having a good time, even if it's freezing out here."

He stares at her. "Are you going to call the police?"

"No." Margot hands him the thermos. "I'm going to help you get these presents wrapped. You take a break and warm up, and then we can move your little operation into the store." She motions for the next person to step forward as she pulls out a length of wrapping paper.

The man blows on his hands before unscrewing the top of the thermos. He puts his face in the steam and inhales. "This smells wonderful, thank you. But why are you helping me?"

"Let's just say it's not great for business if a man keels over from frostbite in front of your store."

The man frowns. "You're joking, right?"

Margot curls a strip of ribbon. "Of course I'm joking. But you have to watch yourself. You're not dressed warmly enough to be sitting here all day. In the very least you'll catch a cold, and who knows, some other guy might set up shop in this space tomorrow." She hands the wrapped present to the customer. "Next!" she calls out.

A man steps forward. "Just this," he says holding out a small, tell-tale square velvet box.

"Some lucky girl's going to be very happy," Margot says as she trims a piece of wrapping paper to fit. She's going to make this one extra nice.

The man smiles. "Yes, I think so."

They wrap a few more presents and then move the table and supplies into the store. They're busy for the rest of the afternoon, with customers lined up out the door, and plenty lingering and shopping inside as well. When the phone rings and Shari tells them that the latest weather report says that everyone needing to go home, so they finish up a few more customers then turn the sign on the door from OPEN to CLOSED.

"I don't know how to thank you," the man says as he starts to gather his things. He's used up all of his wrapping paper, and they ran out of tape an hour ago, Margot having contributed a few rolls of her own. "Oh, here's your thermos back. Thank you." He holds it out to her.

Margot waves her hand. "Keep it," she tells him. "Consider it an early Christmas present. I ended up with some new customers, but really, it was fun."

"It sure was," Shari says. "I have to go get Layla now. If we're not snowed in, would you like me here tomorrow?"

Margot nods. "Nine o'clock, if that works for you. That'll give us some time to prepare for another busy day." She turns to look at the man. "You, too, if you want. I can make room for you in the corner of the store, right over there."

He's holding the poinsettia plant in his arms. "That's very generous, but I won't be here tomorrow. I'm only in Avalon for the day."

"The day?"

"My name is Kevin Faulks. I'm a reporter with the *Chicago Tribune*." The man grins. "I'm sorry I didn't tell you sooner, but I honestly didn't mean to deceive you. It's just that I'm writing a story about the spirit of Christmas and for a while there, I was worried that my editor was right."

Margot is perplexed. "Right about what?"

Kevin smiles. "That the spirit of Christmas is a thing of the past. You were the first person not to threaten me or call the police. I had one guy kick my table—that's why the leg is bent over there. Another shop owner trampled my plant." He nods to the sad-looking poinsettia in his arms. "I've been doing this in eleven towns throughout the state and Avalon was my last stop. Did you know that more people here offered to pay me or make some kind of donation? One lady brought me a sandwich and another came back with a small bag of cookies. And then…you." His eyes are shining.

Shari is beaming and Margot is at a loss, not sure what to say. "Well…" she says, flustered.

Kevin holds out his hand. "I guess all that press about Avalon being the friendliest town in America is true after all."

Margot shakes his hand and then pulls him in for a hug. "Well, you fooled me, Mr. Faulks, and you taught me a lesson or two as well. Merry Christmas." Her eyes are wet as she pats him on the back. Then she pulls away, wiping her eyes. "Oh dear, I'm not going to be in the paper, am I?"

"Yes, ma'am. Unless you don't want me to name you or your store, that is. I can keep it anonymous." There's a twinkle in his eye.

Margot clears her throat. The *Chicago Tribune!* "Do whatever you think is best," she says.

Kevin grins. "I will. Goodbye."

They all walk out together and on the sidewalk part ways—Kevin down the street to where his car is parked out of view, Shari to the elementary school, and Margot home. She's still in a daze when she walks through the door.

"There you are!" Gordon rushes forward. He's dressed in an overcoat with only one boot on. "Why weren't you answering the phone? I didn't know if you heard about the weather. I was about to come down and get you myself!"

"Oh, it was bedlam. I've had…quite a day. I'll tell you all about it but I think I need to sit down first."

"Cider?" Gordon offers.

"I've had my fill of mulled cider. Just some hot water, thank you, Gordon." Margot drops into a plush armchair with a sigh. Gordon has a fire going, and she tosses in a couple of pinecones, a hint of eucalyptus filling the room as the pinecones pop and crackle.

Gordon returns with a mug of hot water and a sugar cookie. "Thelma Talley brought a tin by," he tells her. He sits next to her. "Margot, I was sure getting worried."

"Oh, don't be ridiculous," she tells him. "I'm fine— always have been, always will be. You don't need to worry about me."

"I want to worry about you," Gordon says gently. He pulls something from out of his jacket pocket. "I was going to give you this on Christmas, but, well, here it is." He holds it out.

It's a present, wrapped in familiar paper. A square.

Margot stares at the paper, remembers tucking in the corners and taping them down. "Where did you get this from?"

"Well, I'm not about to give that away," Gordon chuckles. "Man's gotta have some secrets. It was just delivered this afternoon."

"This afternoon?"

He nods. "Not too long ago, actually. Are you going to open it up or are we going to sit here talking about it all day?" He grins, and then goes down on bended knee. "Hurry up now—you know I have bursitis in my knees something awful and I have something I want to ask you."

Margot doesn't have to open the present to know what's inside. She throws her arms around Gordon's neck, her heart bursting with love.

"Yes," she breathes. "I do."

Raffle

⌒

"To date we have forty-four vendors signed up, our highest number ever." Eula McGuire, chair of the Avalon Christmas Bazaar, taps the clipboard with flourish. "Art work, handmade craft items, jewelry, hair accessories, clothing, baby items, candles, and too many baked goods to mention. We'll have live music and one of the residents from Harmony Homes has agreed to be this year's Santa Claus. The butterfly class at Avalon Montessori will be dressing as elves."

The women gathered in the sitting room at Madeline's Tea Salon offer a small round of applause, but Eula holds up a hand.

"I'm not finished yet," she says, her voice firm. "The booth fees just barely cover our cost. We make money by selling raffle tickets which, to date…" she checks her notes then finishes dryly, "we've only sold ten." She gives everyone a stern look. "*My* ten."

There's a stir. Hermina Hooper raises a hand. "I have six people who said they were interested," she tells the group. "They just haven't paid me yet. But they will. I think."

"And Lars and I plan to buy our tickets this afternoon,"

Veronica Ericksen says, casting a nervous look around. "And I might be able to buy a couple extra tickets, too. I just don't know yet."

"Well, I've already pre-sold my tickets," Lynn Armstrong says. "I just have to get the money from everyone."

"That's the same with me," Geneva Burch says. "My entire raffle booklet of ten is spoken for."

"Spoken but not paid for," Eula points out. She tells the group, "If they express an interest, you need to collect the money right away. Otherwise they might never follow through."

"I've never been very good about asking people to buy tickets," Mary Lou Calhoun says with a sigh. "It just seems so pushy, you know? I figure everyone knows about the bazaar and knows that we're selling tickets. It just seems easier if they come to us."

"I've had a few complaints," says Dorothy Clements with a sniff. She's a secretary at Gunther & Evarts, a small architecture firm. "Everyone's saying the price increase is too much."

Eula puts her hands on her hips, incensed. "We only increased the raffle tickets by a dollar!"

"Well, a dollar is a dollar," Helen Welch points out, nodding towards Dorothy. "Money doesn't grow on trees, after all. I myself won't be buying more than two."

"Way to show your support, Helen," Tammy Rutledge mutters. She's standing in the back of the room with her arms crossed.

Helen whips around to glare at Tammy. "I am showing my support! I'm buying two tickets! Did you and Steven even buy your tickets yet?"

Tammy's face turns beet red. "That's none of your business!" she snaps. "Who asked you, anyway?" She glares at Helen.

"All right, all right," Eula says. "Let's just calm down. The holidays can be a stressful time for people—I understand that. But the whole point of the bazaar is to bring a little holiday cheer to every Avalonian while raising money for a good cause. I think we all agree that a community medical center is long overdue. Goodness knows I appreciate the hospitals in Freeport and Rockford, but we need to have more services here. We're lucky that Dr. Richard knows how to pull everything together to make something like this happen but we need to do our part by helping him raise the funds. Five thousand dollars will help him hire the right people to get contracts in place and fundraise for even larger sums of money so this dream can become a reality."

There's a murmur of agreement. There'd been talk for some time about building a small facility in town, one that would cover Avalon and the neighboring towns of Barrett and Laquin, but no one knew how to begin. When Dr. Richard Johnson moved to Avalon almost two years ago, the talk finally became action. All they need now is the money.

"So," Eula continues, "I'm counting on each of you to do your part. Think about the emergencies that could be stabilized if we had a facility right here. It would save lives. Think about those of you who have a hard time driving or finding someone to drive you to Freeport for routine outpatient surgeries or checkups. Now it'll be less than five minutes away. Think of all the pregnant mothers and children who could be treated right here in town. Think of your spouse, the people you care about. Think about yourselves. This could dramatically improve the quality of life for the people in this town.

"So sell your tickets, have your friends and neighbors

sell tickets. If you can, buy more than one. Everyone will have a chance to win some wonderful prizes, but more importantly, it'll bring us one step closer to our goal of having a medical center right here in Avalon."

There's a burst of applause as the women start talking eagerly, inspired by Eula's speech. The bazaar is less than two weeks away and Eula knows that momentum is important. If you can't get the ball rolling, you might as well give up.

"To refresh your memory, here are some of the prizes," Eula reads. "There's a weekend getaway in Chicago, hotel and meals paid, for two people, courtesy of Enid Griffin over at Avalon Travel."

"Oh, I'd love to win that," Veronica tells her neighbor. "I'd love to get away with Lars. Does it come with babysitting?" She and Lars have twin eight-year old boys.

There's laughter and Eula chuckles. "Avalon Sunshine Hardware is giving away garden baskets worth forty dollars each to three runner-ups. Avalon Grill is offering a dinner for four, not including alcohol. Margot at Avalon Gifts 'N More has donated two fifty-dollar gift certificates."

"Has anyone smelled those new gardenia candles?" someone exclaims. "It's just like the real thing!"

"The Avalon Book Nook is giving away a basket of hardcover bestsellers," Eula continues. "Lucy Pavord has donated one of her custom birdhouses as featured in *Country Living*, and Hannah Wang is offering a package of ten cello lessons. We have lots of small prizes, too, like free car washes by Hank Maloney. Little Gracie Evarts is baking two loaves of Amish Friendship Bread, you choose the flavor. Jacob Eammons will walk your dog for one week and the junior class at Avalon High will wash two of your cars once a month for the rest of the school year. There are lots of other things, too, and..." Eula stops, her brow wrinkled.

"That's funny. I don't recall this prize." She squints at the paper, holds it up to the light as if it's written with invisible ink.

There's a curious hush. "What is it?" somebody asks.

Eula looks at Alberta May, the event co-chair. "Alberta, do you remember any last minute raffle prizes?"

Alberta May shakes her head. "Just what you mentioned, Eula."

Eula frowns. "Well, I typed this list myself," she says, "and I don't remember this last item." She reaches down for her purse and pulls out a pair of reading glasses. She slips them on and looks at the paper once again, the same look of confusion on her face. "I must be getting crazy in my old age."

"For goodness' sake, Eula, are you going to tell us what it is or do we need to march up there and read it ourselves?" DeeDee Spitz looks exasperated. DeeDee is the owner of the Avalon Dance Studio.

"All right, all right," Eula says, flustered. "For this raffle prize, the winner will receive…" She takes a deep breath. "…their rent or mortgage paid for one year." She takes off her reading glasses and rubs her eyes.

There's a stunned pause, and then pandemonium. Checkbooks appear as if out of nowhere, with offers to sell any remaining raffle ticket booklets.

"Hold on, how do we know this isn't a hoax?" Tammy Rutledge demands above the din. "I mean, who donated this prize? Is there a name? A number? How do we know this is real?"

"Tammy, don't be a sourpuss." Helen turns to Eula and holds out two twenty-dollar bills. "Eula, tickets, please!"

"Oh, now *I'm* the sourpuss?" Tammy asks, her arms crossed. "You didn't even want to sell tickets a minute ago, much less buy one for yourself!"

Helen just ignores her.

"There's a phone number here," Eula notes. "But no name. Honestly, I don't remember this one at all." She scratches her head.

"A year's mortgage? Eula, how could you forget?" someone asks.

"She's had so much going on with the bazaar, do you blame her?" someone else says in Eula's defense.

"Let me call," Tammy volunteers. "I'll get to the bottom of this." Her eyes are blazing and she looks ready for a fight.

"No, no, I'll call," Eula says. "After all, I am chair of the Avalon Christmas Bazaar." She looks at the expectant faces around her. "What? Now?"

"Well, of course now," Dorothy says. "I want to find out if this is the real thing."

"Me, too."

"And me."

There's vigorous head nodding. In fact, it's clear to Eula that they won't be able to move forward with any other bazaar business until she makes the call. How that prize got listed on the sheet, she has no idea, but she wants to find out, too.

"Fine," she says. She pulls out her cell phone and carefully punches in the numbers. Honestly, the numbers are so small on these phones that Eula doesn't know how people don't make more mistakes. She presses the button for the speaker phone and the room quiets the minute the phone starts ringing.

"Harmony Homes, this is Kelly. How may I direct your call?"

"Harmony Homes?" Veronica Ericksen says. "The retirement community?"

"Senior residential facility," someone corrects.

"Oh, sorry. Wrong number." Eula disconnects the call

and looks at the other women, bewildered.

"Well, that was strange," Helen says. "Henry and I looked into putting his mother over there, but she didn't want to leave Grand Detour."

"Maybe you misdialed," someone suggests.

Eula checks the number. "Nope. I got it right."

"I bet one of the residents did it as a hoax," someone else suggests. "Some of them, you know, aren't all there."

"That's not a very kind thing to say," Alberta says, frowning. "It could be any one of us in there. We're luck to have our health, both physical and mental. I know that's one thing I'm grateful for."

"It still doesn't explain how it ended up on Eula's sheet," Geneva Burch points out. She shakes her head. "No, there has to be another explanation. I'm going to buy some more tickets, just in case. Even if it doesn't turn out to be real, the money is going to a good cause, right?"

"Right," Lynn Armstrong says. "And there are all those other wonderful prizes, too." She digs in her purse and comes up with some cash. "Eula, I'll go ahead and spot those raffle tickets for my friends, and then pick up three more tickets for myself."

DeeDee Spitz rips a check from her checkbook and walks it up to Eula. "I'm going to buy tickets for all of my instructors," she says. "I know a couple of them are going through a rough time. This could help them out if they win."

There's a flurry of activity as more women take their money to Eula for tickets.

"But it's not real!" Tammy bursts out as the women walk back and forth. "We don't have any proof that this is a legitimate prize!"

"So what if it isn't?" Helen retorts. "I'm willing to take my chances. You never know."

"That's my point—we *don't* know, Helen." Tammy spins

around to face the group. "We can't go around promoting this prize without being able to verify if it's real. It's misleading. And what happens when someone thinks they might have won it?"

Eula lets out a deep breath and waves the last person away. "Tammy's right. We don't have any proof. It's such a big prize, and a generous one, that if someone won it and it turned out to be a hoax, they'd be crushed." She clears her throat, her pen hovering over the paper. "Well, I guess that's it, then. I'll just cross it out."

She's about to draw a line through the item when someone calls out, "Wait!"

It's Virginia Miles. She's a spry thing, a young widowed mother with a child, a sick child. She doesn't have a chance to participate with many community events because she's often home with Julie, her four year-old daughter who has a rare blood disorder. The medical center would mean a lot to Virginia and her daughter, who would be able to be treated for routine procedures right here in town instead of driving the long distances they've become accustomed to.

Virginia's face, usually pale and drawn from exhaustion, is pink with excitement. "What if it isn't a hoax?" she asks. "I mean, what if it's real?"

"Oh goodness, Virginia," Eula says. "For all I know I wrote it in my sleep. Wishful thinking."

"But what if your wishful thinking somehow made it real?" Virginia persists. "Or if it just *is* real?"

The women of the Avalon Christmas Bazaar committee look at one another.

"You can't pretend that something's real when it's not," Tammy tells her. "That's called lying."

"Tammy Rutledge, did you wake up on the wrong side of the bed this morning or what?" Helen snaps.

"But what if…" Virginia says, walking around the room,

"...what if this *is* an actual prize?"

"That would be a Christmas miracle," someone says with a sigh. "I would love to not worry about my mortgage for a year."

"Or our rent," someone else says. "I could relax about money a little more. Not feel so anxious, like what I'm doing isn't enough, or that I'm always playing catch up."

There are nods.

"Remember how tight things were for many of us a few years back?" Mary Lou Calhoun says quietly. "I hope never to go through that again. Len and I almost got divorced."

There's a sniffle in the crowd. "Stan and I did divorce," Cassandra Simon says, her eyes wet. "We were fighting about money all of the time. It wasn't just about the money, of course, but I like to think that if we hadn't had the mortgage and everything else hanging over our heads, we would have had a chance at working on our problems."

A few hands reach out to rub her back. Hermina Hooper gives Cassandra a hug.

"Look, all I'm saying is that it can't hurt to believe that we have this great prize," Virginia says. "Even if it doesn't turn out to be true, it makes me hopeful that anything is possible."

"Please, it's too ridiculous for words," Tammy scoffs. "You're delusional. Someone paying your mortgage for a year? You actually believe that?"

Virginia turns to face her. "Yes, Tammy, I do. Even if you don't."

Tammy just shrugs. "Go ahead and believe whatever you want," she says.

"You know, I will." Virginia sits down and opens her purse. "Many of you know I can't afford a raffle ticket—I can't afford much these days with our medical bills and my part-time work schedule since I need to be home with Julie.

But here." She fishes out several wrinkled dollar bills, smoothing each one in her lap. "This should cover it. One raffle ticket please, Eula."

"Now, Virginia, there's no reason to let Tammy pressure you into buying a ticket," Eula says, shooting Tammy a look. "We know things are tight for you and Julie, and we appreciate the time you take away from her to help us plan the bazaar."

"I'm here because I want to be," Virginia says, looking at everyone in the room. "I appreciate what all of you are doing to try and bring more medical services to Avalon. I want to do whatever I can to help. So here." She holds out the money again. "I would like one ticket, please. It'll be fun for Julie, too. It'll be nice to have something to look forward to, to be honest." She gives a small, embarrassed smile.

There's a quiet stillness in the room, words and emotions put on hold. Everyone, even Tammy, seems to be lost in thought, their faces no longer filled with tension or excitement or sadness. Something in the room has shifted, everyone's earlier concerns or opinions about this or that having evaporated, and in its place, a sort of understanding.

Virginia waits, holding out her money.

Dorothy Clements is the first to speak.

"Put your money away," she says, burrowing through her own bag. She comes up with a fistful of bills. "I was going to buy a ticket." she confesses to Eula. "Eventually. May as well do it now. And I'd like to give it to Virginia."

Virginia insists. "Oh, that's not necessary, Dorothy…"

"Me, too." Lynn Armstrong says. She pulls a ticket from the ones she just bought from Eula and hands it to Virginia with a smile. "I hope it's a winner. Good luck!"

"Here," Helen Welch says, passing one of her tickets to Virginia as well.

DeeDee Spitz does the same. Mary Lou Calhoun as well.

Soon every member of the Avalon Christmas Bazaar Committee has purchased and donated a ticket to Virginia. Every member, that is, except Tammy Rutledge who's clutching the straps of her purse with a white knuckle grip, her lips set tight.

Virginia is sitting in her chair, her lap filled with tickets, her eyes shining. "Thank you," she says to everyone. "Thank you, thank you."

"You're sure to win something," Geneva Burch says. "Maybe even more than one prize." The other women nod and smile.

"Well," Eula says, wiping her eyes. "That was certainly unexpected." She checks her list. "And it looks like every remaining ticket is spoken for—you all have either purchased or promised to sell what was left of the tickets. If every ticket gets sold, we'll have enough money for Dr. Richard to start the project. We still have a ways to go, but it's a good first step."

"Showing that the community is behind the effort will help us," Alberta May tells everyone. "It shows community support. It'll help Dr. Richard raise more money when he's writing grants and approaching other donors."

"We can do it!" Helen Welch says with a burst of confidence. "We'll make it happen. We can do it!" She pumps her hand in the air, triumphant, and the room is filled with cheers and applause. A few of the women hug.

"Thank you, everyone," Eula says, beaming, when she spots something on the ground. She bends down to pick it up. "Huh. It looks like we have one ticket left," she says. She holds it up.

"Please," Virginia says. Eula sees that she's still holding her money. "Please, may I buy that last ticket?"

"Well, sure," Eula says. "I don't see why not."

Virginia smiles as she walks to the front of the room to

give Eula her money. Eula hands her the ticket. Then Virginia turns to come back, but instead of returning to her chair, she walks straight to Tammy Rutledge.

"Here," she says, holding the ticket out. "This is for you, Tammy."

Tammy's face drains of color. "Me?"

Virginia nods. "Everyone should have a chance at the raffle," she says. "Even if you don't believe. Yet." She grins.

Tammy reaches out and takes the ticket. She stares at it for a long time.

"We still have more bazaar business to cover," Eula says. "But let's take a break first. Madeline has set out some tea and finger sandwiches in the dining room for us. Ten minutes, all right?"

The women chatter with excitement as they exit the sitting room. Soon it's just Tammy and Virginia, staring at each other silently.

"So," Tammy says.

"So," Virginia says.

Tammy clears her throat. "I don't know what to say. Steven and I…" Her voice breaks but she forces herself to continue. "The bank just foreclosed on our house. Nobody knows."

Virginia just smiles. "Maybe this will be the lucky ticket then," she says.

"And the kids…they're not going to come home for Christmas. Eileen has to work through the holidays and Danny wants to be with his girlfriend. We haven't even met her yet." Tammy presses her lips together, tries not to cry.

"So come spend Christmas with me and Julie," Virginia offers. "We could use the company—the holidays are always lonely for us. People are usually so busy with their families so it's just us. I'm going to cook that free turkey I got from the Pick and Save."

"I got a ham," Tammy says, sniffling. "And stuffing. I could bring that."

"Julie makes a sweet potato puff with marshmallows," Virginia says, nodding. "So long as you're not diabetic, it's delicious." They begin to walk towards the dining room.

"So I have to ask," Tammy says. "Do you really believe, Virginia, or were you trying to make a point? You know, because it's Christmas and all, and it's better to look on the bright side of things…"

Virginia slips her arm through Tammy's and just smiles, a twinkle in her eye. "Come on, let's eat."

Cookie Exchange

✍

"I THINK THIS BELONGS TO YOU."

Erin Meeks looks at the stranger's outstretched hands, at the broad smile on the woman's face. The woman is holding her monthly subscription of *Get Fit* magazine.

"It was sent to my address by mistake," the woman explains. "I live three blocks away, at 2145 Gerbera. But this is…" She checks the faded wooden numbers on the side of Erin's house and then looks at the address on the magazine. "2415 Gerbera. Well, an easy mistake, isn't it? In fact, I'm surprised it hasn't happened more often."

Erin manages an awkward smile as she reaches for the magazine and accepts it, embarrassed. She already has a wicker basket by the door that's already filled with past issues of *Get Fit*, *Slim Slimmer Slimmest*, *Skinny Woman*, and other health and weight-loss magazines that Erin has yet to read. Every time she opens one up, she gets so discouraged that she has to close it again.

"Oh, wow. You must like to exercise," the woman says, noticing the overflowing basket. "It must be youth. You young people are so good about staying active."

Erin's cheeks redden. She's in her mid-thirties, about forty pounds overweight, and despite her growing stack of fitness magazines, she doesn't like to exercise.

Erin works from home and has bought every piece of exercise equipment she could afford. Most of it's sitting in the garage, gathering cobwebs, the steel spotted and rusting, the rubber grips cracked and peeling from hot summers and freezing winters. Erin's woken up at the crack of dawn, forced herself to walk a mile in the wind and rain, and for what? Another pound on the scale, that's what.

She wants to blame Oliver, her ex-fiancé, but what would be the point in that? It's not like she hasn't had to live with her decision to cancel the wedding (on the *day* of her wedding) every day for the past two years. It's one reason she escaped Duluth for Avalon, put a state between them. She gained forty pounds and the last she heard, he was engaged to Carly Gisler, her cousin and former maid-of-honor.

She had broken it off because she knew he was cheating on her, but more importantly she knew that she didn't want to be married to him. Yes, it would have been nice if she had figured that out earlier, but sometimes you don't know until the answer is staring you in the face. That was what had happened—she was walking down the aisle when she saw Oliver looking at her, his face tight and pinched and resigned like the women in her fitness magazines. That's when she realized that he didn't love her, and she didn't love him. They were getting married because they'd been engaged for years and neither of them knew how to break it off.

So she did.

Since then she's had to field complaints from her parents, her former almost-in-laws, the neighbors, even her so-called friends who thought she was crazy to give Oliver up.

Work became unbearable. Seeing people became unbearable. It just seemed easier to hole herself up and keep her own company so she quit her job and started working from home, selling antiques online. It took her six months to put on the weight and now, eighteen months later, trying to lose it has become a battle that's left her weary and discouraged.

Does Erin like to work out? No, she does not.

"I keep meaning to go on a diet," the woman continues. "But now, with the holidays…" She grins at Erin, giving her a helpless shrug. "I have a weakness for peanut butter snickerdoodles dusted with cinnamon. I think it was Martha Stewart who first turned me on to them. I just love Martha, she's just so clever, don't you think? And Rachael, too! Her thirty-minute meals are my favorite, but this month's feature on cookie exchanges was inspirational. It gave me lots of ideas for what to do for mine."

Erin forces a polite smile—she finds it a bit odd how people call celebrities by their first names, as if they were friends. "I don't really read those magazines," she admits. It's too much temptation, too many gorgeous photos of food that she knows translates into a zillion calories. "Well, thank you for bringing this by."

The woman catches the door just as Erin begins to close it. "I was thinking—any chance you'd like to come to our cookie exchange? We do it every year, and we're always saying how we'd like to get some young blood in the group. It's so much fun and I'm hosting this year."

"A cookie exchange?" Erin gives her a doubtful look. A cookie exchange is the last thing she needs right now.

The woman nods. "We each bake three or more dozen cookies and then swap them. You end up with such a wonderful selection of cookies to bring home, it's better than anything you could buy at the store. Great for holiday entertaining, or for those late night munchies, you know? Carl—that's my husband—and I sit in front of the fire, a glass of warm milk for him, a cup of tea for me, and look through the cookie tins like it was Christmas. Which, come to think of it, I guess it is…"

"Thank you for the invitation, but I don't eat carbs," Erin says. She feels a twinge of discomfort because this isn't true. She does what she can by not keeping any in the house, but she's been known to buy a sleeve of mini donuts and down them in her car. Like yesterday. And the day before that. "I mean, I try not to." She nods down at her body, as if this were explanation enough.

The woman looks at her, blinking, and it's clear that she isn't quite sure what that means. "Oh," she says. She stares at Erin's body and squints.

"Anyway, I should get back to…uh…" Erin makes a vague gesture towards her living room where her laptop has most likely gone to sleep. "Well, thank you again."

"Anytime," the woman says. She claps her mittened hands together then waves goodbye as Erin closes the door.

Back in the living room, Erin drops onto the sofa. She has a pair of tin and pewter mirrored wall sconces that she needs to shoot images of and package up, and she'll need to re-do the lights in her makeshift studio before she can shoot a trio of Fenton hobnail lamps that she found at an estate sale last week. All these things need to be done, and more, but instead Erin turns her attention to the papers and charts scattered on the floor. It takes her a moment to figure out where she left off, but then she finds it.

She picks up a ruler and begins to connect the dots on her weight graph, looking for any patterns. She's always heavier in the beginning of the week because of the weekend. She turns to another piece of paper and makes some notes, reducing her caloric intake on Saturdays and Sundays by two hundred and fifty calories. She lops off another fifty calories a day to make up for the donuts. And the hot chocolate with whipped cream that was calling her name after she'd sold a Wallace sterling silver charger tray the other day. Erin studies the chart one last time before capping her pen and sighing.

That should do it.

The next day, an unexpected front has blanketed Avalon. Erin wakes and looks out the window. Her backyard is a vision of white, a fluffy meringue. Tree branches seem to be piped with royal icing, fondant drapes the ground. Spun sugar hangs from the eaves, the stone garden statues transformed into marzipan figurines.

She doesn't regret calling off the wedding, but she does regret that she never got to eat her wedding cake, three tiers of luxurious sugar roses with rippled petals and sugar pearls that rivaled the real thing. When she'd suggested to her parents that they eat the cake anyway, her father had grown livid, and thrown the cake into the trash.

Erin goes into her kitchen and opens the refrigerator, pulls out a carton of eggs. She'll make herself an egg white omelet with a tablespoon of salsa on the side. After breakfast she'll do some sit ups, then put in one of her exercise DVD's. The rest of her morning will be spent online—it's the time of year where people get desperate for a little spending cash for the holidays and try to unload things they've been holding on it. She'll be able to build up her inventory for the first part of the year over this next week alone.

She's about to crack an egg into a mixing bowl when there's a heavy thud coming from her front doorstep. She puts down the egg and listens for the doorbell to ring or for someone to knock, but everything is silent once again. She wipes her hands a dishtowel then walks to the front door.

It's early, just shy of seven.

She looks through the peephole but doesn't see anyone. She opens the door and almost trips over a tall stack of magazines, tied with heavy twine, a note tucked underneath. Small footprints leading to and from her doorway dot the snow.

Wrapping her robe tighter around her body, Erin breaks the seal on the envelope and pulls out a stiff note card.

LADIES, TURN ON YOUR OVENS!
IT'S TIME FOR THE ANNUAL COOKIE EXCHANGE

Bring three dozen cookies of your choice
to share and swap.
Appetizers and hot beverages will be served.
Sunday 2:00 p.m. at the home of Gerri Evans
2145 Gerbera Avenue

Below is a scrawl:

No need to bring anything! Just you! xx G

There's a faint scent and Erin raises the invitation to her nose. Cinnamon. She remembers what the woman—Gerri—said about the peanut butter snickerdoodles and feels her mouth being to water.

It takes several good lugs to pull the bundle of magazines inside. It's so heavy that Erin doesn't bother to drag it past the entryway. How on earth did Gerri manage to carry these? Erin tugs on the twine and the knot falls away, the magazines slipping from their neat pile and onto the floor.

It's a year's worth of *Martha Stewart Living, Everyday with Rachael Ray,* and *O, the Oprah Magazine.* Magazines Erin refuses to read, because they seem frivolous, almost dangerous. One look and all her careful planning and dieting will be gone in a second.

And yet...

She reaches for the first magazine, a spring issue of *Martha Stewart Living*. Brightly colored Easter eggs in a palette of pastels, a splash of color and sunshine, green grass, smiling faces. An Easter buffet spread out on a long wooden picnic table dressed with fresh cut flowers. A crispy pear galette, frosted sugar cookies, chocolate bunnies. Quiche, a generous salad, lemonade. Sunshine, laughter, children running through the green grass in their bare feet. A far cry from the cold and bleak winter they're having in Avalon.

Erin picks up another magazine. A chili cookout, pictures of families and friends gathered together and chopping onions, tomatoes, peppers. Fat wedges of cornbread that look so right on the plate that Erin doesn't even bother to think of what the fat or calories might be. An oozing apple pie with a perfectly browned lattice crust.

In another magazine, the spread falls open to a birthday party. Women her age, a few that even look like her, surrounding a large cake with candles too numerous to count. What Erin notices isn't the bowls of Swiss chocolates or parfaits lining the buffet, but the stacks of presents, the smiles, the laughter. Friends.

Erin finds herself devouring every page. Not just the food, but the stories of real people who look happy, carefree. She's hungry, but it has little to do with food.

The hours slip by. Erin still sits on the floor by her door, a cup of tea nearby, reading. At times she even finds herself smiling, turning down the corner of the page, making a mental note to herself. Try this or that? Check this website, maybe, or that new book? A blouse that might actually look good on her, and those boot cut jeans, too. Erin reads every page, every line, looks at every picture. Even the pictures of food don't bother her anymore, but make her consider the possibilities. Half a portion, maybe, or exchanging sugar with stevia or agave? What would freeze well, be easily portioned for one?

It's dark by the time Erin gives a stretch and a yawn, stands up to go to bed. She hasn't had dinner, only nibbled on some raw carrot sticks and hummus. She's not hungry, but comfortable. Erin knows she can't live on raw carrot sticks and hummus, but for now she's fine to go to bed with nothing more. Nothing more than a mind full of inspiration and a plan to call Gerri Evans in the morning.

"Ladies! Ladies, this is Erin Meeks from twenty-*four*-fifteen Gerbera!" Gerri Evans is beaming as she introduces Erin to the ladies. "Erin, these are the ladies of block twenty one!"

There's a friendly twittering. "We heard about what happened!" someone exclaims, clasping Erin's arm as if it were more than just a wayward magazine. "How funny is that?"

Erin manages a smile even though her heart is racing. What is she doing here? Her nose is ruby red from the biting wind and her feet are half-frozen from the walk over. It hadn't been her choice—her car wouldn't start and she didn't want to be late so she trudged through the snow, three plastic containers filled with chocolate and vanilla pinwheel cookies with a crunchy peppermint twist. She found the recipe in one of the magazines Gerri had given her, lulled by the words *quick* and *easy*. And it was.

Her kitchen was filled with the most delicious aroma. She fretted, knowing that she might devour each and every cookie as soon as the oven timer went off, blowing both her diet and her contribution to the cookie exchange. But when the baking pans came out of the oven and the cookies looked as perfect as promised, she found herself reaching for her camera instead. Instead of eating the cookies as she had feared, she spent the next hour snapping pictures— arranging the cookies on plates, napkins, stacking them in a clear glass jar. She tucked them into cupcake liners, then later let some spill from a wicker basket lined with a festive dishtowel. When she'd counted out three dozen, she still had a couple dozen left over. She wrapped these up in small jam jars to give to her neighbors, figuring that there was no better time to reach out than the holidays. She suddenly didn't want to keep to herself anymore.

And the truth was that she was showing off a bit. Erin was used to taking pictures of the antiques she'd re-sell on eBay, where the right lighting and angle could affect the final bid price, but this was different. She was proud of what she'd done. She made these cookies, and was now sharing them, and more importantly she wasn't scarfing them down like she did whenever she went on an eating binge. No, she'd savored the three cookies she'd eaten. Took her time, enjoyed the crisp crunch of the cookie and peppermint pieces, the soft center, the taste of warm dark chocolate on her tongue. It was satisfying, and when she finished the third cookie and thought about reaching for a fourth, she decided against it. It felt better to save them for others, so that's what she did.

But now, standing among all these women, Erin feels shy. Self-conscious. She's all layered up which makes her feel even bulkier. But at Gerri's instance, she shrugs off her puffy down jacket, her scarf, her mittens, her woolen hat. Gerri waves her in the direction of the "coat room" which turns out to be her bedroom. Inside, Erin sees that Gerri's bed is already stacked high with jackets and adds hers to the growing pile.

Back in the kitchen and living room, Gerri is organizing the cookie exchange like a drill sergeant.

"Put the name of your cookies and your own name on these display cards," she tells everyone. "NEATLY. And I have a packaging station with tags, labels, ribbons, boxes, scissors, and tissue paper so you can wrap your cookies up nice or give them away. Coffee and tea are on the counter, help yourselves. Luz, don't eat the inventory yet! I also have snacks in the living room. Erin, can you help get Luz a plate?"

"But I don't know where—"

"Thank you, dear," Luz says as she snakes another gingerbread tree. "Just load me up with whatever Gerri's made for us. Nothing with celery, though. I am definitely *not* a celery person."

"She needs celery," Gerri tells Erin. "Doctor Richard says it helps lower her blood pressure and cholesterol. Make sure she gets a few stalks."

"No! No stalks!"

"Okay, but—" Erin begins again.

Gerri points to the living room and gives Erin a gentle push, frowning when she catches Luz hiding an orange peel thumbprint cookie into her napkin. "Luz!"

In the living room, Erin makes a plate for Luz and then for Alana, one of the women who seems to be Gerri's second in command. As the first round of women choose their containers and then their cookies, Erin finds herself looking forward to her turn. She won't eat the cookies, of course. She'll just be participating to be courteous. Oh, who's she kidding?

When her turn comes, Erin is almost faint with the possibilities. Lemon icebox cookies, chocolate-dipped shortbread, candied stained-glass wreath cookies, Mexican wedding cakes, caramel cookie bars, pecan bars, macaroons, chunky chocolate chip, oatmeal cranberry, chocolate gingerbread bars, molasses sandwich cookies...

"Well, go on," Gerri says as she stands behind Erin with her own empty tin. "They're not going to jump into your container by themselves. And you know you get to mix and match up to three dozen, so go for it!"

Thirty six cookies? Erin can sense her negative script coming up, right on time. That she shouldn't eat these cookies. That she shouldn't even think about it. That she *should* be home with her spinach and chicken breast. That she should be exercising. And on and on.

"Hush," she says aloud, and reaches out to pluck a chocolate chip coconut bar to put in her box. When another negative thought comes up, she shushes that one, too, and adds a sugar cookie decorated with red and green sprinkles.

"Are you talking to me?" Gerri asks, confused, then smiles when Erin picks up several of her snickerdoodles.

A few minutes later, Erin's box is full and tied with a bright red ribbon, a small silver ornament dangling from the knot. She already knows she's going to shoot pictures the minute she gets home.

"It looks like some of us overbaked this year," Gerri says, surveying the remaining cookies. "Which is perfect, because I was thinking: I love our cookie exchanges, but we should share them with others. What do you say we fill a few extra boxes and bring them to the folks at Harmony Homes?"

Heads are nodding. "I was thinking the same thing," someone else exclaims. "And you know what else? We could bring treats every week. Not just for the holidays, but throughout the year. If we divvy up the weeks among all of us, we'd only have to bake three or four times a year. I mean, we all love being in the kitchen, right?"

"That's an excellent idea," Luz says, cookie crumbs gracing the corners of her mouth.

"Let's go for a show of hands," Gerri suggest. "If you've got too much on your plate, don't worry about it. But if this sounds like something you'd like to do, we can do it together. All in favor?"

Erin looks around at the women, all of whom have their hands up, women whom she's just met and is eager to get to know. She's one of the younger ones, but that doesn't bother her. On the contrary, she likes the idea of being around women who may have some wisdom to impart.

But baking on a regular basis? The thought of keeping flour and sugar and chocolate chips in the house feels both dangerous and liberating. Should she risk it?

She sees herself walking to Gerri's on a regular basis, her weight slipping off, her laughter coming back. She sees herself cooking, experimenting. More photos, more recipes, more possibilities. All the fitness magazines in the trash, the fitness equipment donated. Meeting someone new. Walks in the park. Candlelight dinners. Like the generous spread of cookies in front of her, Erin realizes that life has a lot more options that she was willing to see.

"Me," she says. She puts her hand up, raises it tall and high, making sure she's seen. "I'm in."

Late Bloomers

"WHAT'S IN THE BOX?"

Jack Studebaker, 62, leans over the garden fence to peer into the snow-covered yard of Bonnie Fisk, his neighbor of approximately the same age. Bonnie is huddled in her jacket, a thick scarf wound around her neck, and clutching a simple pine box in her hands. She's staring at a frozen patch of ground. "It's Fred."

"What?" Jack reels back, horrified.

Bonnie looks up and he sees the twinkle in her eye as she lets out a gay laugh. She flaps a mittened hand at him. "Of course it's not, silly. Fred's buried over at the Avalon Cemetery. You were at the funeral, for goodness sake!"

Jack's head suddenly feels hot beneath his woolen cap. That's right, he was. It had been a somber affair, because Fred had gone for a run one morning and dropped dead of a heart attack somewhere near Main and Azalea. They were all in their mid forties at the time. Fred and Bonnie had two teenage children who've since upped and moved to the city.

"You got me," Jack says good-naturedly, but he looks at the box warily.

"I just found it hidden under all the junk in my garage," Bonnie tells him, turning her attention back to the ground.

"Spring bulbs. Tulips, I think, or maybe hyacinths. Must have been left over from a planting." She nods to a corner of the yard that is always abundant with flowers come spring. He can see it from his back living room window, and in May it's like he's gazing at a painting, full of color and life.

Jack's yard is mostly dirt and rock. He'll get the occasional comment from one of the more prim neighbors down the street, but he's not spending his Sundays mowing the lawn or pulling weeds, no sir. He doesn't have to spend money on fertilizer or seed or a lawn mower. He doesn't have to water or worry about tree roots ruining the foundation of his house. He knows his yard's not much to look at, but really, who's looking? That's the one thing he figured out long ago, way before most people. If you do it for yourself, that's one thing, but if you're doing it for another person, for show or approval or whatever you want to call it, you're like a dog chasing its own tail. It's a pointless pursuit.

"It's nuts, I know, but I'm thinking about putting these in the ground," Bonnie says. Her breath comes out in little white puffs. "I mulched this spot good and right before winter set in, before the snow. There's a small chance I might be able to break through any frozen dirt and bury them deep enough so they don't freeze."

"Sure," Jack says. "But, no offense, why bother?"

Bonnie gives a slow nod as she places a gloved hand on top of the box. "I know," she admits. "It doesn't make much sense at all. I'm not even sure how old these bulbs are." She pushes some snow aside with the toe of her boot. "And yet…"

Jack waits, curious.

She looks at him. "And yet I think I might do it anyway." She shrugs. "I've got nothing to lose, after all. Worse case scenario, they don't come up. No real harm done, right?"

"Except the we're freezing our butts off just having this conversation," Jack points out. He's never been one to mince words. It was what his younger brother said to him almost three decades ago. *That's the one thing about you Jack. You always say whatever's on your mind, even if it ends up hurting other people.*

As true as that was, Jack had been stung by those words, the last conversation they would have. He'd been loyal to Everett since they were young boys, known to family and neighbors as "those Studebaker Rascals." It had always been said with a wink and a smile, even when they burned down a neighbor's tool shed by accident or plowed into a row of mailboxes when they put their mother's idling car from PARK to DRIVE and stepped on the gas. Even as they got older, Jack two years Everett's senior, they were more than brothers, they were good buddies. They served in the army together, married within a year of each other, and helped each other out without so much as a thought.

And then Jack and his wife split, later followed by Everett and his wife. Jack had figured that this was how things were meant to go, and now the Studebaker Rascals were on the loose again. But before they could even hit a bar, Everett broke the news that he was set to remarry. It hadn't even been three months.

"It's Gwen," Everett told him. Gwen was Jack's ex-wife, a beautiful woman Jack had fallen hard for, only to find that she didn't feel quite the same about him. When she finally told him that she didn't love him anymore, they were married and five years of his life had passed. He'd broken a lot of furniture in the house, yelling and swearing, and Gwen had left in tears. Good riddance, he'd thought.

But now Everett was telling him that he and Gwen—Jack's Gwen—wanted to get married. They were in love, had grown close while Jack was finishing up his last year in the service. Gwen had always been Jack's girl, and it had been assumed that they would marry. Everett had married after, wanting to put it all behind him, but had failed. Gwen, too. They wanted to be together now, and they wanted Jack's blessing.

"Hell no," he'd said. He was still in disbelief. Had Gwen cheated on him? No, Everett assured him. Until now, they'd never shared so much as a kiss. Still, Jack felt betrayed.

"This isn't personal," Everett began, but Jack cut him off.

"If you want to get together, it's your head, not mine," he said. "But give you my blessing? I'd rather shoot myself in the foot and then walk ten miles to the emergency room. That seems like a lot more fun, little brother, then watch you make the biggest mistake of your life. You can come crawling back later, but until then, I have no intention of setting foot into any house that has her in it. Don't even think about calling me until she's gone."

And that had been the end of that.

Everett and Gwen got married and moved across the state. The divorce Jack was sure would come never did.

For a long time, there was nothing. And then when Jack's mother died twenty years later, Jack saw them at the funeral with their three children. It had been a shock, it was true, and Jack felt his long-held anger begin to fade. Middle age helped—Everett was paunchy around the stomach, probably one too many donuts, and had fallen to a headful of early grey. Gwen, fortunately or unfortunately, was as beautiful as ever but there were wrinkles around the corners of her eyes and mouth. Even though they were at a funeral, you could tell they were happy. One of their kids, a high school-aged boy, kept sneaking looks over at Jack. He reminded Jack of himself somehow, a bit irreverent with an unforgiving cowlick, a troublemaker. Jack had chuckled and, at that moment, it had seemed like enough.

When Jack's father died two years ago, he saw them again at the funeral. All of Everett and Gwen's children had married and now had children of their own. They were ten people strong while Jack was still a party of one. Gwen and one of her daughters-in-law kept passing a baby back and forth, a little girl. The baby slept throughout the service and, as if on cue, woke up at the very end with a yawn and stretch, her fists curled into little balls. Jack felt his breath catch. He had to blink away tears.

He tried to catch Everett's eye, but Everett had stared straight ahead, unwavering, his eyes fixed on the pastor, and then, later, the lawyer. Only Gwen had turned to look at him with her gentle green eyes, not with anger or resentment or even bravado. She only looked sorrowful, and had offered a small, kind smile. It just about ripped him up.

Jack feels a pang at the memory. The truth is that he hasn't been able to put them out of his mind, and he doesn't know the first thing about how to end this thing that he has started. If he took his life and divided it right down the middle, there was life with Everett and life without Everett. Almost the exact same number of years.

Bonnie hands him the box. "Hold this," she instructs him now, then turns to reach for a shovel leaning against the fence. There's a distinct *clunk* as the shovel hits frozen ground.

"Well, shucks, if you're going to go for it, let me help," Jack says, straightening up to his full height. He's easily twice her size. "I mean, I can do more than hold this damn box."

Bonnie gives him an amused look but taps the ground with the head of the shovel, refusing to hand it over. "Thank you, but this is something I'd like to do," she says. She lets out a delighted gasp when the shovel finally slips into the ground a couple of inches. "And look, just like I told you. Ground is softer here, right where I added all that extra mulch."

Jack watches as she breaks up the frozen mulch and digs up the cold earth. He stamps his feet to keep warm.

"I really don't get what all the hype is about with gardening," he says. "It seems like a big waste of time. And I thought you were supposed to get the winter off!"

"A garden is never finished," Bonnie quips, grunting. Her small frame is putting everything she's got into the task before her. "Plus it's nice, Jack. Seeing something grow over time. Nature is quite incredible, you know. If these bulbs are meant to come up, they will—we just have to help them along a little, that's all. They certainly can't plant themselves. Not these, anyway." She stands back for a moment and leans on the shovel, catching her breath. "I have a good feeling about this, Jack. Think about the story we'll be able to tell next spring—we were standing in the frozen yard right around Christmas, planting bulbs like a couple of crazy people!"

"*You're* planting the bulbs," Jack clarifies. "Make that crazy for one. I'm just holding the box."

"Everyone has their part," she says. She bends down and digs into the soil with her gloves. "Okay, I think this is enough. Hand them to me, one at a time."

Jack watches as Bonnie carefully takes each bulb and places them in the ground, then covers them up again, using some fresh soil from a burlap bag nearby.

"The snow actually acts as in insulator," she tells Jack as she finishes up. "The earth isn't frozen solid like a lot of people might think. It was even muddy in some parts." She pats the earth with the shovel. "There. All done."

She shakes out the empty box and hands it to him. "A present. From me to you."

He stares at it. "What am I supposed to do with an empty box?" he asks.

"You really don't have any imagination, do you, Jack?" Bonnie says as she gathers the shovel and bag of soil. "Here's what I've learned about boxes. They hold things."

"I know what boxes do, Bonnie. I just don't have anything to put inside." He knows he's sounding ungrateful but the truth is, he doesn't want this box. He doesn't want clutter or anything unnecessary in his house—he prides himself on the fact that his life is straightforward and simple, just like him. "That is, everything I own already has a place. It's not like I have stuff sitting around waiting for an empty box to show up."

"Now you're talking nonsense. When I found the box this morning, I thought it was full of letters. I used to keep letters from Fred in there, you see, from when we were courting all those years ago. I'd forgotten that I moved them to a safe deposit box, and must have tossed these bulbs in without a thought. It was a delight to see them just the same—it reminded me of how life goes on, and that's why I couldn't wait to put them in the ground."

"Well, I don't have any old letters or flower bulbs."

"Then pass the box along, for goodness' sake! Surely someone you know might find a good use for it. It's a shame to just throw it away, but I can tell it's ready to leave my home for another." She starts to lug her things back to the garage. "Merry Christmas, Jack. I've got eggnog and you're welcome to come by anytime, even though I know you won't."

"I might," he ventures, but Bonnie just chuckles and gives him a friendly wave as she disappears around the corner of her house.

Back inside, Jack is muttering as he turns up the heat, trying to warm himself up. If he just throws the box away,

Bonnie won't be any wiser. Who the heck could he give the box to, and what on earth would be put in it?

He places the box on the small table next to a shelf of photo albums. He hasn't looked at the albums in a while but can't bear to throw them out, either. He settles into his brown Naugahyde recliner, the artificial leather cracked and worn thin after years of use. He'd bought one for him and one for Everett when they'd turned 30 all those years ago, saying they were growing up to be just like their dad. It was the one piece of furniture he couldn't break when Gwen left, because it was too heavy and bulky and awkward. Next to the albums, it's one of the only things he has left that reminds him of the past.

Jack reaches for one of the albums. 1979. He remembers that year and a smile breaks across his face. He was twenty eight, Everett was twenty six. They were both still married then, and they'd all gone to see the Cubs play the Phillies at Wrigley Field. It was May 17th, the final game in a three-game series.

The weather had been great, sunny and bright, really windy. They were all in good spirits having made the drive from Avalon, laughing and huddling together as they made their way to the stadium. Only Jack and Everett were baseball fans, the women coming along for the ride and the promise of shopping after. The air was sizzling in anticipation, and Jack knew something big was about to happen.

It was the most spectacular baseball game he'd ever witnessed, in person or on TV. Jack remembers balls being hit out of the park, the crowd roaring, all of them screaming and jumping in the air as the game went from inning to inning, ten in all. In the end, the Cubs had lost 23-22 and as disappointing as that was, Jack knew it was a day he'd never forget.

Gwen had put their pictures of that day into this album, including their tickets and other memorabilia. The pages are stiff as Jack looks turns them, one by one. In all the pictures they are happy. *Happy.* When Gwen left him he thought of throwing them all in the fire, but he couldn't bring himself to do it and now he's grateful for that restraint.

There are more pictures from the summer of 1979, of barbecues and hikes through White Pines Forest State Park. And that fall, they visited the Yerkes Observatory to see the stars. Then Christmas, Jack and Everett standing before the tree in matching sweaters, their arms around each other's shoulders, grinning. The Studebaker Rascals.

When he reaches the end of the album, Jack knows what to do with the box. He wipes it clean and then reaches for the albums, carefully removing his favorite pictures. Then he reaches for a piece of note paper and begins to compose a letter that's been long overdue.

Dear Everett,

I hope this letter finds you well. I am fine, still living in Avalon. Still selling insurance. I have high blood pressure and had hip replacement surgery a couple years back. Can't see worth a damn without my glasses. Can't complain otherwise.

I was looking through my photo albums today and thought you and Gwen might like these. I don't know what you've told your kids about me, or if they even know about me, but I thought they might like to look at pictures of their old man and his even older brother in their glory days.

Well, that's it from me. Please give my regards to Gwen.

Jack

P.S. I got this box from my neighbor who tells me it should be passed along, whatever that means.

P.P.S. If you want to call or get together sometime, I would like that. I don't have much in my house but my neighbor always has egg nog and I'm sure she wouldn't mind if the Studebaker Rascals went over and spiked it with some good rum or bourbon. Gwen and the kids are welcome, too.

It's hardly Shakespeare, but it'll do. Jack thought about saying how all is forgiven, but it was half a lifetime ago. To bring it up now would be looking back, and Jack's not interested in going that direction.

Jack tucks the letter into an envelope and reaches for his jacket. He'll take the box and the letter to the post office and mail it, hope that Everett and Gwen haven't moved. He still has their address from the lawyers a couple years back.

He opens his front door and stands stunned for a moment. Fresh snow is falling, fat flakes eddying lazily from a bright white sky. He looks up and wonders if it's too late. Two old men making up after all these years. And then he thinks of his neighbor, of the flowers that will be blooming in her yard in a few short months, that even though it is quiet and barren now, the flowers are there, patient and waiting for their turn. He thinks of Bonnie's willingness to step into the cold and plant in the unlikeliest of weather, optimistic that the bulbs will bloom and willing to take the chance even if they don't.

I've got nothing to lose, after all. Worse case scenario, they don't come up. No real harm done, right?

But if they do come up, her tulips or hyacinths or whatever they are, she'll have the rest of the season to enjoy them. Those flowers will be doing exactly what they're meant to do. Human nature, Jack decides, is not so different. Resilient, hardy. At the time he'd acted in the only way he knew how, but now it's a different time, a different season. He thinks of the picture of him and Everett standing in front of the Christmas tree, and clutches the box to his chest, eyes closed. He knows this is more than mere sentiment, but a deeper desire to reconnect, a willingness to change an old pattern that doesn't serve him. He's struck by an odd, unfamiliar feeling, one spoken by his neighbor an hour before.

Hope. Optimism. And a feeling that this might just work out.

And We're Wassailing

❦

THE KITCHEN TIMER DINGS. Bartholomew Solomon slips on his worn oven mitts, then cracks the oven door and takes a peek.

The breadcrumbs are crisp and golden. Underneath the crust Bartholomew knows the thyme, garlic and cloves have mingled with juicy red tomatoes, bacon, kielbasa sausages, pork and white beans resulting in a scent so enticing that Bartholomew has to resist grabbing a spoon and taking a bite right there. No, he has to wait.

He brings the cassoulet to rest on the stove. He's tinkered with it over the years, experimenting with different ingredients and flavors. Sometimes he'll go traditional and throw in a few duck legs, other times he'll use lamb. He's halved the recipe, he's doubled it, he's made it vegetarian with leeks and carrots. He's made the recipe at least one hundred times, has taken home two blue ribbons from different cooking contests. This dedication may seem admirable by some, but Bartholomew knows it's only because he's a lonely man with too much time on his hands.

He reaches for a loaf of French bread and begins cutting it into thick diagonal slices. For those ten years he was married to Margie, all Bartholomew could think about was how he'd give his eye teeth for a little peace and quiet, for a chance to do the things he loved. Margie was more of a homebody and she balked whenever he wanted to grab his fishing pole or join his buddies to bowl a couple frames at the Avalon Gutter. Married life was dreary and predictable and he often found himself wondering what it was that made him propose in the first place. The baby, of course, plus everyone around him was getting married. It seemed like the thing to do, the next logical step in life, you know?

But he hadn't thought it would be so confining, someone always sharing your space, the loss of independence so deep it felt akin to losing a limb. He dreamed of being on his own again, and when Frankie was nine, he got his wish. Bartholomew and Margie divorced, and she took Frankie with her. Suddenly the house was empty, and Bartholomew was finally alone.

Margie has long since remarried. Frankie's a college dropout, working at the dock for the Port of Chicago. They talk a few times a year, each conversation strained and uncomfortable, but still Bartholomew is sad to hang up, longing for a few more minutes of mumbled pleasantries, of long awkward silences, of anything. He'll take whatever Frankie's willing to give, but Bartholomew knows that it may be too late. He wasn't there for Margie and Frankie when it mattered most, and now they're not there for him. He can't blame them for that.

What he wouldn't give to turn back the clock, to have the house filled with voices and bodies and stacks of dirty dishes in the sink. All the things that bothered him before, the small details that remind us that we're never alone, that our lives and our spaces are shared and meant to be shared. He didn't get it before, but he does now, and that's what he wants more than anything. To be included in a life other than his own.

The doorbell rings just as Bartholomew finishes setting the table. His heart is racing and his mouth is dry, his armpits damp with sweat. *Don't mess this up, don't mess this up,* he thinks as he hurries to the front door, almost tripping on a snag in the carpet. He's a big man and he feels himself pitching forward, his weight pulling him towards the floor, but he manages to catch his balance and right himself.

"Hi…" he begins as he throws the door open. There's a blast of cold air and Bartholomew blinks, registering the sight in front of him.

Ten smiling faces, adults he's seen around town but doesn't know, sheet music in hand. They're dressed like they're out of an old-fashioned book complete with bonnets and top hats, the women's hands tucked into woolen mufflers.

Not exactly who he was expecting.

"Greetings!" The leader of the group beams gaily at Bartholomew, his breath coming out in little puffs of smoke. "We're caroling for the holidays and would like to sing a song to bring you a little Christmas cheer. And a-one, and a-two, and a-…"

"Not now," Bartholomew tells them. He looks down the street and sees the headlights of a car turning the corner. "Please go. Hurry!"

The carolers give him a perplexed look.

"We can make it a quick one," the leader offers. His name is Keith Greene. During the day he repairs phone lines for the local telephone company, but at night he leads practice sessions of the Avalon Octaves, a mixed group of a cappella singers. "What about *I Saw Three Ships?*" Keith raises his index finger and begins to tap it in the air like a baton.

"I saw three ships come sailing in, on Christmas Day, on Christmas Day…" the Octaves begin singing.

"No, no!" Bartholomew waves for them to stop. "I have to ask you to leave. I'm sorry." He closes the door, his heart pounding. He goes back to the table and straightens a place setting, rubs a smudge off the tine of a fork.

A few seconds later there's a knock on the door again. Bartholomew takes a deep breath. "Walk, don't run," he tells himself. "You're both adults. Everything will be fine." He takes his time going to the door, then takes another deep breath before opening it.

"Hi, it's me again," says Keith Greene, his voice apologetic as he pokes his head through the gap in the door. He gives a slight wave. The rest of the Avalon Octaves are standing on the sidewalk, keeping their distance from Bartholomew, their eyes wary. "I just wanted to check—did you want us to *go* go, or go for now and then come around again later? Because we're going to circle the block and then cross the street, then circle the block again, sort of in a figure eight, which means we'll end up right back here…"

"Do whatever you want," Bartholomew tells him. "Just leave right now, okay? I don't want to be rude, but I'm expecting someone very important any second."

"I understand." Keith grins. "It's that time of the year, huh? We'll wish you a merry evening, then!" He tips his hat.

Keith leads the Octaves into a rousing rendition of "Carol of the Bells" as they head down the sidewalk. Bartholomew just shakes his head as he closes the door.

He casts another look around his living room. It's plain, an old man's bachelor pad, no plants or color to speak of. He meant to get a tree, but it seemed like overkill, like he was trying too hard. Plus he'd have to buy ornaments. At the time it seemed like an unnecessary expense but now Bartholomew wishes he'd splurged. He might never get a chance like this again.

The doorbell rings and Bartholomew turns, his hand

already on the knob. He hopes it's not that caroling group again, because some very un-holiday-like words are on the tip of his tongue. He pulls himself tall and sucks in his gut, then opens the door.

"Happy holidays!" comes the cry. It's his neighbor from across the street, Flora Goodman. She's at least twenty years older than Bartholomew, a widow and an eccentric. Twice he's caught her watering her plants with his gardening hose, the water turned on full blast. Another time she was rifling through his mail. She's a terrible driver and has knocked over his trashcans more than once on garbage day.

Now Flora is holding out a dense-looking bread dotted with raisins and wrapped in plastic wrap. "I did a little holiday baking!" she announces. "Rum Raisin Amish Friendship Bread, emphasis on the rum." She drops it into his hands and it feels like it weighs at least five pounds. Flora stands on her tiptoes and tries to peer into the house behind him. "Boy, something sure smells good!"

Bartholomew blocks the door. "I'm having people over for dinner," he tells her, his voice blunt. "It's not a good time, Mrs. Goodman. But thank you for this."

"What? I'm not *giving* it to you, Barty! I just wanted to show you. Though I'm happy to share a slice if you care to invite me in—I'm gonna glaze it with honey, I think." Flora gives a sniff. "What is that divine smell?"

"Cassoulet," he says, handing her back the bread.

Flora tucks it under her arm like a football. "Your famous cassoulet, huh?" she says. "So who's coming for dinner? Anyone I know? Someone important, I bet."

Bartholomew hesitates, then gives in. "It's Frankie."

Flora lights up. "Frankie, your boy?" she asks. "No kidding. How old is he now?"

"Thirty one."

She whistles. "Time sure does fly. Is he married?"

Bartholomew shakes his head. "No, but he has..." He clamps his mouth shut, not wanting to say more.

Flora raises an eyebrow, waiting. "Go on."

Bartholomew hesitates, then bursts out, "He has a three-year-old son. Riley. I'm going to meet him for the first time today." It's a relief to say the words aloud, to share the news. Frankie only told him about Riley a couple months back, and Bartholomew had begged to meet him. Now, at last, they're coming for dinner and Bartholomew can't wait.

"Frankie's a dad." Flora marvels with a click of her tongue. "Imagine that."

"So I'm sure you understand that I have to go," Bartholomew says, scanning the street. "They'll be here any minute and I want to be ready."

She nods. "I hear you. It's nice to have people with you for the holidays." Flora thumbs in the direction of the carolers who are making their way from house to house. "I can't wait until they get to my place. I'm going to request three songs: *Twelve Days of Christmas, The First Noel,* and *Deck the Halls.* It's a classic—you can't have Christmas without that one."

He nods, anxious for her to go.

"It's going to be my last Christmas here, you know," Flora continues. "Heading to Harmony Homes just after the new year. Yep, that's going to be *fun.*" She rocks back and forth on her heels, nodding a bit too enthusiastically.

"Oh," Bartholomew says, surprised. He knows Harmony Homes is some kind of senior living facility. "I'm sorry to hear that, Mrs. Goodman."

Flora knits her brows. "Mrs. Goodman? Come on, call me Flora—I'm only a couple years older than you!"

More like a couple decades, Bartholomew thinks, but asks, "What about your house?"

"Bank's taking it," Flora says. "I kinda got behind on my

payments. The money Joe left me ran out a long time ago and, well, a gal's got to eat, right?"

"Right." Bartholomew shifts uncomfortably. "Well, happy holidays."

"I've overstayed my welcome. I get it." Flora sighs. "Okay, Barty, see you later. Swing by anytime if you want a slice of this bad boy." She hefts the loaf above her head like a trophy and leaves.

The phone rings just as Bartholomew closes the door. He hurries to answer it, thinking that it must be Frankie, that something has happened.

"Hey," comes Frankie's voice, sounding strained and far away.

"Frankie!" Bartholomew does his best to sound upbeat. "Everything's ready—the cassoulet just came out of the oven and I got you that French bread you liked the last time you were here. It was baked fresh today, they told me. And the carolers are going around the neighborhood. You think Riley might like that?"

"Look," Frankie says. "I'm sorry, but I don't think we're going to make it to Avalon. The traffic…"

"Oh." Bartholomew's face scrunches up like he's about to sneeze. He knows Frankie can't see him but he forces a smile anyway. "Well, I'm in no rush. You could come tomorrow—it tastes even better on the second day, you know. I mean, whatever works for you and Riley."

"Tomorrow's not going to work, either." There's a heavy sigh. "Riley goes back to his mother's and I have to work. I think we'll have to skip this year. Riley's being a handful right now…"

"I can help," Bartholomew offers. "Just come, and you can relax and I can keep him busy. Give you a break."

There's a snort. "A break?" Frankie says bitterly. "Seriously? I see him twice a month for less than twenty-four hours, and that's in a good month. Riley hates being with me. I'm as much of a bang-up father as you are."

Are. Present tense, not past. Frankie's accusation lingers in the air between them, each word a pointed barb, a poison arrow, and Bartholomew feels struck.

"Frankie," he begins, not sure of what to say but his son cuts him off.

"No," Frankie says. "I just want to get through this night, and driving out to Avalon isn't going to help."

"I could come out," Bartholomew offers a bit desperately. "I can pack everything up, be there in a few hours…"

"Riley'll be asleep by then," Frankie says. "And his mom is getting him in the morning."

"Oh. Well, okay then." Bartholomew swallows. He wants to reassure Frankie that maybe it's just a phase, those terrible two's and three's, but he doesn't know if that's what is is.

Frankie sighs again, and Bartholomew can almost see him, his son tall and lanky, knobby muscles and dark brown hair that needs to be cut, trying to console his own son who wants nothing more than to go home to his mother, his toys, his friends.

"Maybe we'll see you next year," Frankie finally says, his voice softer now, a little sheepish. "Sorry for the trouble."

"It's no trouble," Bartholomew is quick to reassure him, putting his own disappointment aside. He's had his time for being selfish, and he'll do whatever it takes now to make it easier on Frankie. "It's okay, son. I understand."

There's a long, painful pause.

"Yeah," Frankie says. "Look, don't take this wrong, but I'd prefer it if you'd stop calling me. For now. I just have a lot going on with Riley and work. I just…I'll call you when I'm ready." He hangs up before Bartholomew can say goodbye.

Bartholomew listens to the dial tone, to the carolers singing outside, their voices muffled. He replaces the receiver on the hook and sits down heavily in his overstuffed armchair, his heart aching.

So that's that. Frankie's not coming, which means Riley, his grandson, isn't coming either. It means that things aren't okay between him and Frankie, and that maybe they never will be. They're doing the best they can, but the damage has been done. All these years he's been hoping they've moved past it, that by not bringing up the past they can focus on the future.

He brings his fingers to his eyes but feels the tears leak out anyway. He was an absent dad, he wasn't there when Frankie needed him. Bartholomew gets that, and he sees this cancelled evening for what it really is, that Bartholomew won't just be passing another holiday alone, but quite possibly the rest of his life.

The aroma of his cassoulet wafts in from the kitchen, reminding him that he now has more food than any one person can eat, that his table is full of misplaced optimism and hope. He wipes his eyes then stares into the white space in front of him, wondering what measure of time will ever allow for forgiveness, if such a thing is still possible. He can wait, or…

Bartholomew picks up the phone. He has to clear his throat several times, almost doesn't trust himself to speak. His mouth is dry. He's not sure if this is a good idea, or if it will change anything, but at this point, he has nothing to lose by trying. His finger skims the worn leather address book by the phone, Margie's from all those years back, until he finds the number he's looking for.

"Hello," he says when the person on the other end picks up. "It's Bartholomew Solomon. Turns out Frankie won't be able to come over after all, and I have all this food…"

"I'll be right over!" comes Flora's eager reply.

So fifteen minutes later, Bartholomew finds himself seated at the chipped dining room table with his neighbor, a woman he's never taken the time to get to know, serving her a generous portion of cassoulet. The rum raisin loaf rests on a cutting board in the kitchen, their dessert. When the knock on his door comes, Bartholomew jumps up and hurries forward, anxious to throw the door open.

"Happy holidays," he says to Keith Greene and the Avalon Octaves before Keith has a chance to say anything. "Could you start with the *Twelve Days of Christmas*, please? And then we'd like to invite you in for a little something to eat or dessert. If you want."

Keith looks surprised, his nose bright red from the cold. Then he grins and gives a hearty nod.

"We'd love to," he says, and claps Bartholomew on the shoulder in thanks. He taps his finger in the air and the Octaves break into chorus, smiles on their faces. Bartholomew hears an enthusiastic, off-key voice joining in from behind him. He feels his heart, still wounded and broken, slowly begin to mend as his once empty house is suddenly filled with people and song.

Winterberry Wreath

JOANNE STUCKEY LOOKS AT the pile of mangled shrubbery at her feet. She puts her hands on her hips and frowns.

"So," she says to the young boy standing in front of her. "What have you got to say for yourself?"

The boy looks down. The flaps on his earmuffs are worn and he's wearing winter boots a size too small, and they pinch his feet. He runs a toe along the icy snow. His toboggan is still tangled in Joanne's winterberry hedge, the bright red berries crushed and glistening.

"I'm sorry?" he says in a small, uncertain voice.

Joanne sighs and gives a shake of her head. Children these days have no manners, and she blames the parents. No one says *please, thank you, may I,* or *excuse me* anymore. No sir, they just go about their business without any consideration for anyone other than themselves. How many times has she seen this one bike by without so much as a wave or hello? He and his mother are renting the small red house down the street, having moved in a couple of months ago. They keep to themselves but Joanne sees him wandering around by himself, his head always down.

"Wanna try that again?" she asks as she wrestles the toboggan out of the brush. "The apology, I mean." When she bought the house a few years ago, she had wondered why it was so cheap. True, she was concerned that the small hill that sloped into her backyard might be prone to flooding, but heavy rains haven't caused a problem. She was thrilled to have gotten a great deal and enjoyed the privacy the hill behind her house afforded her.

Then the first snowfall of the season hit, leaving six inches of thick, white powder. Before Joanne could blink, the neighborhood kids and their sleds were out, and the hill behind Joanne's backyard became a popular after-school hangout. The older and more experienced sledders were smart enough to maneuver away from Joanne's house and into the empty lot next door. But the younger children could do little more than scream with joy or terror as they found themselves sliding down the hill and stopping a few feet shy of Joanne's backyard. This boy was the first to slide all the way in. If she hadn't planted the winterberry there, he could have ended up in her living room.

Not only that, the stone birdbath was less than three feet away and could have caused some serious damage to both the toboggan and the boy. And lucky for him Joanne chose to plant rows of ilex verticillate winterberry holly instead of the more traditional ilex aquifolium holly with the prickly glossy leaves. That would have most certainly scratched him up some.

Joanne shakes some stray branches and snow from the sled. It's scuffed and beat up, and the leather strapping worn thin, the tow rope frayed. But it's a nice sled, made from ash wood, carefully crafted by hand. She gives a whistle.

"This is some sled," she says handing it back to him. "When I was your age, my friends and I used to slide down the big hill behind our school on plastic trays we swiped from the lunchroom." It's a good memory, and Joanne smiles.

The boy's head is still down but he manages a small nod. She's about to turn and leave when she hears him say, "I'm sorry for ruining your bushes, miss." He sniffles and brings the sleeve of his jacket up to his nose.

Joanne knows she has a reputation in the neighborhood for being a bit reclusive, especially the past year. She has never been one for groups or neighborhood events, but her own life demanded her full attention and she didn't want to explain this to anyone, didn't want anyone's help or sympathy.

"Apology accepted," she says. "Just be careful next time. I don't want to have to take you back in pieces to your folks, okay?"

The boy gives a sniffle again and it takes her a moment to realize that he's crying.

"Oh, hey now," she says. "You didn't ruin them…exactly. See? There's still some good pieces here I can use." She makes a small bundle of branches at their feet then she points down the row of winterberry. "And all of these are in good shape, too. I'll be able to use all of it, so buck up. It's no big deal."

The boy wipes his eyes. "So what are you going to use them for?" he sniffles.

"Wreaths," Joanne says. "At least, that's the plan. I haven't made any yet. I've been dreaming of making one, and then I got busy and…well, I just got busy." *Funny how busy you can get when you're going through chemo.*

"What are you going to do you with a wreath?" the boy asks.

Joanne studies him for a moment. He's slight, but he looks about seven, maybe eight. An easy kid for the others to pick on, to ignore. She doesn't see any other kids around and whenever he walks or bikes to school he's alone. Something about him tells her that he's an only child, or maybe just a lonely child.

"I was just going to make one to hang on the front door," she says. "But I suppose I have enough branches to do a giant one for the garage door, too. Wouldn't that be something? Eye catching, huh?"

The boy nods. "It sure would be. Are you going to do that for sure?"

Nothing is ever for sure, she wants to tell him, but that's a Dr. Phil answer for a question the kid didn't ask. Last fall she was admiring the winterberry wreaths that populated stores and graced doorways, so she made a trip to the nursery. Not even a day after they were in the ground, she went in for a routine mammogram and there it was, a fuzzy cluster of cells gone bad. From there things progressed at a clip: the biopsy, surgery, four months of chemo. The winterberry shrubs, along with most other details of her life, were forgotten.

But now, life is back to normal, whatever that means. Remission. The stoplight of her life switched from red to yellow—*proceed with caution*. They're watching, but it looks good. They caught it early and Joanne is one of the lucky ones, but still her oncologist reminds her that she has to stay vigilant. She has to take care of herself. No stress. Stay positive. She's part of a cancer support group that helped with meals and massages and house cleaning before her infusions and when she was going through the worst of it. She still feels muddled at times, her brain refusing to cooperate, her keys or glasses mysteriously disappearing and re-appearing, her thoughts slow and sluggish. But her good days are becoming more frequent, and today is one of those days.

The boy's nose is running and Joanne's done with the cold weather. "Come on," she says. "Prop your toboggan over there and help me carry these branches inside. I'll get you a tissue."

⌐───────

Inside, they drop the winterberry branches on the kitchen table and Joanne clucks when the boy forgets to take off his boots. He goes back to the door and steps out of them, one at a time. It's then that Joanne sees how wet his socks are. His big toe wiggles from a gaping hole in his right sock.

"Kid," Joanne says, handing him a dry towel. "You could get sick walking around with wet feet." She passes a box of Kleenex across the counter.

The boy blows his nose, a loud honking nose. He balls up the tissue and reaches for another, then looks abashed when Joanne points to the trashcan. He blows his nose again and then throws the discarded tissues away, going to the kitchen sink to wash his hands. "Thank you," he suddenly says, almost as an afterthought.

He may just learn yet, Joanne thinks.

She points to the wall phone. "Do you want to call your mom and let her know you're here so she doesn't worry?" Joanne starts to sort out the wiry branches and berries, the snow already melting into small puddles on the table.

The boy hesitates and Joanne looks up, a brow raised.

"She's not home," the boy finally says in a small voice. "She's at work."

"So call her at work."

"I'm not supposed to call her at work unless it's an emergency. It's not her real job, just a temporary one, so she's not supposed to get phone calls. She says it's a really good job and it helps with the money so she doesn't want to lose it. She says she'll have a surprise for me when she gets back, too. I asked her if it was McDonald's, but she says no. She says I'm just supposed to come home and do my homework and wait until she gets back."

Joanne raises an eyebrow. "When's that?"

"Around seven." The boy looks nervous. "I already did my homework, miss."

"Okay, stop with this 'miss' business. I'm 58, hardly a miss by anyone's standards." She sticks out her hand. "Joanne Stuckey."

His hand is small in hers. They shake. "I'm Hoyt Schaffer. The Third." He sits up straighter in his chair.

"The third? Where's Hoyt Schaffer the Second? Or do they call him Junior?"

At this Hoyt smiles. "Junior," he confirms. "And he's overseas right now. Afghanistan. He gave me that toboggan. It used to be my granddad's."

"And that would be Hoyt Senior, I presume."

Another grin.

"Well, Hoyt Schaffer the Third, while I don't want to bother your mother, I think we should let her know you're here. How about if I call her? Just give her an update?"

Hoyt thinks about this then nods. He tells her the number and she punches it into the phone.

Hoyt's mother, Samantha Schaffer, works at a furniture store in Laquin. After her initial wariness, she seemed relieved to know that Hoyt was just up the street at a neighbor's.

"I know I'm not supposed to leave him at home alone," she apologizes nervously, and Joanne can't help it—she feels herself bristle. She was holding out for the possibility that Hoyt's mother was too frazzled to know better, but it's clear that she does, which somehow makes the act of leaving a child all the more egregious. But there's no point in making Samantha anxious and Joanne doesn't want to get Hoyt in any sort of trouble.

Samantha continues, her voice hopeful, "And tonight I have to…well, I'm going to be late as well, right at dinner time. If he could stay with you until then, I would really appreciate it. I have to go to…well, I'm not quite sure how to explain it…"

"You don't have to explain," Joanne says, cutting her off. She doesn't want to hear any excuses or explanations, she just wants Samantha to know that she's happy to have Hoyt and that Samantha doesn't have to worry. "We'll see you when you get back." They say goodbye and Joanne gives Hoyt a thumbs up.

He lets out such a happy whoop that she can't help grinning, too. "So I'm thinking hot cocoa," she says. "What do you think?"

Hoyt gives an eager nod. "Yeah!"

Cocoa, cocoa, where did she put the cocoa? It's been so long since she enjoyed a cup of cocoa, having turned her own attentions to green and white tea. Her fridge and cupboard are stocked with a host of recommended cancer-fighting foods. Dark chocolate. Goji berries. Grapefruit. Kale. Spinach. Quinoa. Brown rice. Almond butter. Flaxseed. Wild-caught salmon. She doesn't have a problem with any of them, but the thought of hot cocoa with a rich dollop of whipped cream…

Heaven.

She doesn't have whipped cream but she finds a tin of Dutch processed cocoa hiding in the back of her fridge, enough to make two steaming mugs. As the pan of milk warms, she makes a thick paste with the cocoa, sugar, and a little milk. She puts some in each of their mugs as Hoyt watches, intent. When the milk is ready she adds it to their mugs and instructs Hoyt to stir, the frothy white milk turning a rich chocolate brown. His eyes grow large when he takes his first sip.

"Wow," he says.

"Good, huh?" Joanne says. She takes a sip of her own.

While whipped cream or marshmallows would have made a nice addition, this cocoa—and this moment—is as perfect as any she could have hoped for. After what she's been through, Joanne knows that life is in the details. Any sliver of happiness, of ease, of joy or laughter is worth its weight in gold.

They finish their cocoa and she loans Hoyt a thick pair of socks. She turns on KAVL 94.5 FM and hears the DJ, Trick McGaughy, introduce some jazzier holiday music. "This'll put a jingle in your step," he chortles.

They set to work, separating the longer branches from the shorter ones. Joanne shuttles inside and out, a pair of clippers in hand as she trims and clips more branches and berries until they have two large piles. They snip clusters of winterberry and place them in a bowl.

"Now what?" Hoyt wants to know. The sugar from the cocoa has kicked in and he's bouncing in his chair, excited.

Joanne tries to think back to the instructions she'd saved so long ago. It's upstairs in one of her many to do piles, piles she hasn't looked at in a long time. Even now she has no interest in looking at them. She should really just throw them all away, save herself the headache of going through them. If she hasn't needed them by now, she probably doesn't them at all.

"Floral wire," she says automatically, the thought popping into her head. It's an old memory but it feels shiny and new, different. "We'll use it to tie the branches together. But I don't have any."

"Oh." Hoyt looks disappointed, but then brightens. "What about string? Can we use that?"

Joanne grins. "Go look over there," she says, pointing to her kitchen junk drawer. She takes another sip of her cocoa, settles back in her chair. She watches as he pads over to the drawer and lets out an *oooh* when he sees what's inside.

He finds a bundle of jute twine which he brings to Joanne. As she unravels it, he returns to the drawer, plucking out marbles, rubber bands, magnets, buttons. He shows them to Joanne and she tells him to keep them if he wants. He finds an old strawberry basket under the sink and stores his treasures in the basket before returning to the table, ready to work.

They choose several of the longest branches and begin tying them together, bending them gently to form a circle. Joanne remembers that the instructions recommended a wreath form to help with the shape, but she doesn't have that and quite frankly prefers not to spend the money.

"Mine looks crooked," Hoyt says, holding it up. He frowns.

It does look crooked, but Joanne loves it, and she tells him that. "Plus it doubles as a crown," she points out. She plops it on his head and Hoyt runs to the hallway mirror and cracks up when he sees himself.

"King Hoyt," she says. "It suits you." She ties off her wreath. Her wreath is crooked too, but she doesn't care. She knows it will grace her front door. She can't wait to put it up.

They tuck the clusters of berries into their wreaths, and then finish it off with a jute hang loop. They're both beaming, proud of their work. Then Hoyt turns to look at the remaining bramble in the middle of the table.

"We still got a lot left," he says. It looks, in fact, like they hardly put a dent in the large stack of berries and branches. He knits his brows, thinking, then snaps his fingers. "We could make that large wreath for your garage door!"

"We could," Joanne agrees. "But I think I'm good with the one." She nods to her masterpiece, still pleased. "Come on, let's go put it up."

She has to hoist Hoyt up so he can tap the nail into the

door. He hangs it, and they step back to admire their work.

"It looks nice," he says, his voice filled with awe. It takes Joanne a moment to find her voice as well.

"It sure does." Joanne feels her breath catch. It's the only Christmas decoration she's had time to put up. That it's from her own yard and made by her two hands makes it all the better. She'd forgotten that she could do that. In the chaos of the past year, she'd forgotten that she could do a lot of things.

"Wreaths are a symbol of many things, Hoyt," she tells him. "They represent peace, love and harmony woven together. They're symbols of hope."

"Really?"

She nods. "Let's get inside."

But Hoyt doesn't move, just stares at the wreath.

"Hoyt?"

He takes a deep breath. "I hope my dad comes home," he finally says, less to her and more to someone or something else. There's a long pause, another breath, as if he's been holding it in all this time. Joanne feels an ache, for her own parents who passed when she was in her twenties. She adds her own silent prayer as well, for the safe return of Hoyt's father's, for help for Hoyt's mother, for Hoyt's own happiness. For the heck of it, she throws one in for herself as well. For strength. Healing. Love.

She feels a small hand in hers, and they walk back inside.

At the table, Joanne looks at the winterberry. "You're right, there's still a lot left," she says. "But I have an idea."

Hoyt looks up at her and simply says, "Okay." He trusts her. No explanation needed.

They know what they're doing now, and it goes faster this time, the branches bending easily, the cluster of winterberries wedged in the right places, the jute hang tags looped in and tucked out of sight.

When they finish, it's dusk. They clean up, brushing dust and debris into the trash, then sit back to inspect their work.

They've made ten wreaths. One for Hoyt's teacher at school, one for Joanne's therapist and another for Dr. Richard who's been keeping a careful eye on her these past few months. There's a small one for Hoyt's father with the hope that they can mail it to Afghanistan—Joanne promised to look into it after she has a chance to talk to Hoyt's mother. The remaining six are going to all the neighbors on their block. The wreaths can be hung inside or out, on the front door or over the fireplace, can double as a centerpiece with candles or platters of food in the center. Both Joanne and Hoyt agree that they like living in a neighborhood where everyone is friendly and they feel safe. They'll deliver them tomorrow after school if Samantha Schaffer is okay with it.

Joanne orders a large pizza from the Pizza Shack, figures that any leftovers can go home with Samantha and Hoyt. She makes an edamame salad for herself, letting Hoyt pop the green soybeans out of their shell.

There's a knock on the door.

"I think that's our pizza," Joanne says, wiping her hands on a dishtowel. She reaches for her wallet. Hoyt does a little dance, pops a soybean into his mouth, and follows her to the front door.

But when they open the door, there's a gasp, and then tears. Hoyt flies into the arms of his father, still dressed in his Army greens, who kneels on the ground to embrace his son. Behind them, a woman who Joanne recognizes as Samantha Schaffer watches as she sheds her own happy tears. She mouths *Thank you* as Joanne wipes her own eyes with the sleeve of her sweater.

A second later the pizza delivery car arrives. A young pimply guy in a down jacket two sizes too large emerges, a thick wool cap pulled over his ears. Steam emanates from the box as he saunters up the walk. "Got a large pie with all the works," he announces.

Joanne accepts the box and gives him a generous tip because he was witness to this wonderful moment, whether he realizes it or not. The delivery guy pauses long enough to grin at the ten-dollar bill, and then at the people around him as it all sinks in. "Wow, thanks. And welcome home, sir. I hope you all have a Merry Christmas!"

"Merry Christmas," they all echo, and the words ring true in their ears.

Hoyt Schaffer Junior straightens up and steps forward to shake Joanne's hand. Samantha Schaffer follows with a hug, and despite the cold Joanne feels herself melt. Hoyt is clinging to his father, a broad smile on his face.

"I know this is a family time," Joanne says, "so you're welcome to take this pizza home with you. I just made a salad I'd like to give you, too." It'll only take her a minute to make another for herself.

"But I want to show them the wreaths we made," little Hoyt protests. "And we set the table already. Can't we just add two more places? And Miss Joanne makes the best cocoa, mom. The best!"

Joanne sees Samantha flush with embarrassment, so Joanne touches her gently on the sleeve to let her know that it's okay. In fact, it's more than okay. "I would love to have you dine with me," she says. "And Hoyt did a wonderful job setting the table."

"Okay," Samantha says. "That would be wonderful. A relief, in fact. Thank you." She turns to her husband, who pulls her in for a hug and nods.

"I'm starving," Hoyt Junior says. "I've been dreaming about deep dish pizza for months. Thank you."

"Tomorrow would have marked one full year in Afghanistan," Samantha says. "His unit finished their mission early so he was able to come home for Christmas. I found out myself last week—I've been trying to put in as much overtime as I can so we can have extra money for the holidays." She gazes up at her husband. "He's served in the Army Reserves for eleven years."

"One more year," he says, his eyes still on his son. "And then I'll be home for good."

One more year. Joanne thinks back to this time last year. How she's come full circle from the moment of diagnosis until today. She remembers how, just a few hours earlier, she and little Hoyt stood in this same spot, offering up their own hopes.

"Welcome home," she says, and opens the door wide.

Sleigh Bells

"I DON'T BELIEVE IT." Cooper Buck, 48, stares at the piece of paper in his hand. He's standing in front of a wall of post office boxes in the Avalon post office, reading a Xeroxed note telling him that his post office box account has been closed since he didn't pay the renewal fee. Any mail addressed to him will be returned to sender, effective immediately.

Coop groans. Why didn't he just stay in bed this morning? He should have called in sick, spared himself this whole horrible day. He woke up in darkness and dragged himself into the bathroom to find he used the last of the toothpaste the night before. He went to make breakfast and spilled coffee grinds all over the floor. He left his last five dollars on the kitchen table and didn't have any money for lunch.

At work he had to fail two senior drivers, which is always a bummer. Coop knows it's a blow to lose your license, because it represents a loss of independence, of freedom. But the first driver kept rolling through the stop signs and twice stepped on the gas when she meant to step on the brake. The other had a penchant for speed even though Coop kept telling him to slow down. When they hit a patch of ice, Coop thought that was it. He'd die in a twisted heap of metal at the hand of an eighty-year-old man named Boyd with yellow teeth and a felt fedora turned inside out.

His last driver of the day was a teenager who snapped gum while she turned on her signal lights at the right time, slowed to a stop at the intersections, and was able to parallel park with only one small bump against the curb. She passed, but Coop knows she'll be driving with her headphones on, maybe even texting her friends, confident and careless. She was already talking on the phone when Coop signed her forms and pointed to the window where she could get her picture taken.

And now this.

Coop rounds the corner of the post office and sighs when he sees a long line of people, packages in hand, waiting in front of him.

Oh, what does it matter? It's not like they're going to give him an extension, because they have, twice already. And it's not like he gets anything in his post office box other than bills and advertisements. Coop looks at the notice, at the ominous words printed in black and white. How is it that a piece of paper can make him feel so bad? After a moment's hesitation, he tosses it in the trash. Already he feels better.

He steps back outside, burrows deeper into his coat. They'd had a big storm a few days ago and the snowplows have been through, pushing large drifts to the side where they hardened into icy stones speckled with dirt and mud. Hardly a winter wonderland. Many storefronts have festive decorations up in the window, inviting gifts tucked behind the glass, beckoning you to come inside. Coop knows better than to step inside. He's in no position to be spending money right now, and besides, he doesn't have anyone to buy a gift for anyway.

It's his own fault, he knows. All that debt, racked up after years of hitting the tables, his own recklessness costing him more than a few dollars, two failed relationships, a lost job, his own sense of self-worth. For years he felt out of control, desperate to earn back whatever he lost, then overly confident when he won a few bucks. Of course it wasn't just a few bucks here or there—it was thousands of dollars that represented his savings and what little credit he had left with the banks.

But five years ago he stopped cold turkey for a reason he's ashamed to admit to, even now. His mother, a wonderful woman who had loved and cared for him all his life, who believed in him even when everyone was saying he was washed up, had died. Her own meager savings had been given to Coop years ago and he'd lost it gambling, just like he had everything else. When the funeral home called him, he realized he didn't even have enough money to give her a proper funeral. In the end he had opted for cremation, the cheapest option, and couldn't afford to put up a marker anywhere. Her remains are still in the simple urn on a shelf in his living room. Someone had anonymously donated the urn when they heard about Coop's run of bad luck, but it just made him more ashamed. He quit gambling the day he brought the urn home.

He cut up his credit cards, visited the bank which helped him consolidate his debt and he began paying it back, penny by penny, dollar by dollar. He skips meals and anything deemed a luxury—he doesn't even own a television anymore. He still has a ways to go, and in the meantime he's going to have to let a few more things go, including his post office box. The small basement apartment that he's renting won't let him receive mail there either. Maybe this is a good thing somehow. He just has to figure out what it means, exactly, because he doesn't know.

"Mr. Buck!"

Someone is calling his name and he turns to see Pearl Arnold, one of the young postal workers, hurrying towards him. He remembers how she had panicked during her driver's test when an ambulance flipped on its siren right behind her. He assured her that she was doing great and gently directed her to pull over so the ambulance could pass. She was so frazzled that he gave her a few minutes to calm down before they pulled back onto the road. She was otherwise an excellent driver, and passed with flying colors. That was three years ago.

Now she's bundled in the postal office-issued coat, an army green scarf wrapped around her neck. She reaches him, her breath coming out in small puffs.

"I'm not supposed to give you this—we're supposed to send it back since your box is closed—but I saw you and thought that it's just one letter, you know?" She holds out a thin envelope with her mittened hands.

"Thank you, Pearl," Coop says, grateful. He doesn't want her to get in trouble but he appreciates this. He takes the envelope and nods toward the post office. "Now go back inside, it's freezing out here."

"Isn't that the truth?" Pearl says, her nose already red from the cold, snowflakes caught on her lashes. "But I'm glad I caught you, Mr. Buck. Happy holidays." She gives him a broad smile then waves and retreats back inside.

Coop steps into his car, a beat-up old Chevy that's seen better days but still manages to run without breaking down. He turns on the engine and flips on the heat, the front and rear defrosters.

That was nice of Pearl, he thinks. It probably wasn't worth the trouble though. He looks at the envelope and doesn't recognize the return address. A law firm? Bill collectors, or God help him, he's being sued for something or other. He's tempted to toss this envelope in the trash, too, but instead takes a deep breath and readies himself to face whatever it is.

He reads the letter four times before it finally sinks in. An uncle on his father's side? The father who left them when Coop was just a child, leaving his mother to fend for the two of them, never to be heard from again? Yes. Here it is, his father's younger brother who passed last week in a car accident. And Coop, the last living relative, has inherited a small fortune. There it is, a check written out to Coop, his name typed in bold black letters.

Coop sits in his car, the engine idling, the vents blasting heat even though Coop can't feel a thing. His first thought isn't about the money, but about his father. If Coop is the last living relative, then that means his father has died.

He doesn't know what to feel. He's numb, and he knows now that he's alone. Utterly and quite definitely alone.

It's not that he pictured a reconciliation. Once, when he was in twenties, he had tried to look up his father, hitting dead end after dead end. But there was one time, in the Par-a-Dice in East Peoria, when he was at the craps table and looked up into a face that could have been his. The two men had stared at each other, silently sizing one another up, surprised but not surprised. The man could have been Coop, fast forward thirty years. Before Coop found the courage to say anything, the man turned and left. He disappeared into the casino crowds and Coop didn't go after him.

But there was always that knowing in the back of his head that his father was out there, somewhere. That Coop was tied to someone other than himself. And if he were going to be completely honest with himself, maybe he did envision some kind of reckoning, a moment that involved an explanation or maybe even an apology, and on Coop's part, forgiveness. It was folly, he knew, but there it was. And now any possibility of that was gone.

Coop leans against the headrest, clutches the letter to his chest, the check fluttering into his lap. A check that more than adequately covers his remaining debt, that would allow him to buy a new car, move into a decent apartment, even buy a small house. A big house. Two houses, maybe even three. To put up a memorial for his mother, to make a donation in her name. He could sponsor a tree in Avalon Park in her memory—she always loved the white oaks, would gather the acorns each fall and keep them in bowls around her room at Harmony Homes.

His mind starts to fly, and he feels an old familiar urge from the past. The possibilities of what he could buy, of what he could do, of the ensuing financial freedom. *This is it.* This check is his reward for having struggled these last few years, it's a gift for his nobility. It's substantial, yes, but think about what he could do—the real good he could do—if it was even more.

"Stop," he tells himself aloud, but his old thoughts—silent for so long—come back with a vengeance.

Vacations, new clothes, a decent haircut. A girlfriend he can dote on, a lavish proposal, vacation homes, a boat. He's always dreamed of having his own company, and now he has the capital to start one, even buy one.

The check is real. This is not a dream.

It's drawn on an Illinois bank. He could cash it now, be at Harrah's Joliet by dinner. He could have a big steak dinner, then head to the tables. He'll set a limit and only play some of the money—he's not foolish enough to bet it all. Just enough play money to see what happens…

"Stop," he tells himself again, and this time he puts his car in gear. He feels himself break into a sweat. He snaps off the heat, trying to catch his breath. He drives straight for Avalon State Bank and practically runs inside.

"Mr. Buck!" Charlotte Snyder, the head teller, exclaims with a tick of her fingers. "We're just about to close. You got here right in time."

"I need to cash this," Coop says, panting. He slides the check under the cashier's window.

Charlotte's eyes bulge out when she sees the amount. She looks at him in surprise, but there's a softness, too. She knows all about his financial difficulties—she had introduced him to their loan officer and he's been in enough times begging for extensions or waivers of late fees. "Goodness," she says. She runs the check through a machine and smiles broadly when it's clear that it's real.

Coop's mind is bursting with the sights and smells of the casino, the feel of the plush carpet beneath his feet. He can feel the chips between his fingers. It's a struggle to get the words out, but he manages.

"First, I want to pay off my credit card balances," he says. "Then I'll need a bunch of cashier's checks." He racks his brain, all the time fighting an almost inhuman urge to grab the check and run, because what if he could multiply this number? This is no joke. It's a once-in-a-lifetime opportunity. One good bet and he could be a millionaire, easy. Maybe even a multimillionaire...

He tries to recall what he's read in the paper, about the charitable efforts around town, the people and places in need. His hands are shaking as he writes down some more numbers on another piece of paper and gives it to her. "I'd like to ask your help in getting these to the right places," he says.

Charlotte's mouth is pursed in an "O" and Coop can see that he's rendered the chatty teller speechless. It's enough to help him catch his breath, to quell the voices clamoring in his head.

"Are you sure?" she finally asks. "It's a lot of money, Mr. Buck. Don't you want to keep any of it for yourself?"

Coop feels his beating heart start to settle, the rhythm familiar to him once again. "I'm doing just fine," he says, because he is. Less than an hour ago he felt like his life was going down the toilet, but now he knows that wasn't the case. He's made it this far on his own wits, and he knows he can still go a bit farther. This money—this gift—is just that, and he intends to use it that way, too.

He doesn't need a television, not yet at least. And his car is doing fine. A new apartment might be a good idea, one with its own mailbox, so Coop will just have to figure out how to do that. On his own.

But then he has an idea. "I'll keep a thousand," he says, because he's going to do something he couldn't do earlier. Walk into several of the stores in Avalon and buy a few gifts for a place he knows are filled with people who could use a nice surprise. A place that took care of his mom that last year of her life, who did a better job than he could have, that's for sure.

And maybe he will have that steak dinner, only not at Harrah's, but at the Avalon Grill. He'll swing back by the post office to reinstate his box and invite Pearl to join him. After all, without her this wouldn't have been possible.

This money, as wondrous as it is, is a test. Coop knew it the moment his mind started to race and knows that if he doesn't release it now, it could be his undoing. To keep it would set him back after he's come so far. Coop has just proven to himself that he has become the better man he'd hope to be, the man his mother always knew he was.

"Well," Charlotte Snyder says, as she hands him receipt after receipt for each of his transactions. "You are certainly going to be making this a merry Christmas for a lot of people. But I have to say I still don't understand why you're giving so much of it away. After all, Mr. Buck, this is enough to make you a very rich man and we both know what it's been like for you." She gives him a sad smile. "I mean, are you certain you want to do this?"

But for Coop, standing on the other side of the window, he feels nothing but certainty. Certainty about who he is and how far he's come. Certainty that this money was meant to pass through his hands and end up not in the banks of the casino, but the hands of people who could use a break. As well-intentioned as she is, he doesn't expect Charlotte Snyder to understand, because only people who have lived through a debilitating addiction know the feeling of having beat it. And today, standing here, Coop knows that he's beat it. And in Coop's book, that makes him the richest man in the world.

He takes the last of the receipts and tucks them into his wallet, knowing that he will look at these small slips of paper from time to time to remind him. Because that's all life really is, a tally of things done and undone, a measure of a person's life. Now, in black and white, Coop sees the measure of his.

"Yes, Mrs. Snyder, I'm sure."

Scrooged

∽

I F YOU WERE DRIVING BY Harmony Homes, the senior residential facility in Avalon, you might not think twice about the cluster of cars parked in the back or the small groups of gentlemen hunched in their winter jackets and entering the building through the back door with a surreptitious glance around them. Even the time—it's just past eight p.m., with visiting hours about to come to a close—might not seem particularly significant. No, the only thing that might make a passerby curious is that everyone walking into the building is wearing a black top hat.

The men are greeted by their compatriots, a handful of Harmony Homes residents, some dressed in their robes and pajamas, top hats on their heads, too. They wave or clap one another on the back in silence, weaving their way around the narrow hallways of the service area until they enter a storage room, the chairs already set up. Elden Burns is stationed near the door, ready to discourage any unwanted visitors. The look on his face is all business despite the top hat on his head and the silk cravat tucked into the top of his striped nightshirt.

The men talk in low whispers, with chuckles here and there, until Lincoln Schmaltz checks the time and uses his cane to tap a box of canned peaches that's serving as a makeshift table.

"The meeting of the Bah Humbug Club is now in session," he says. "Let's start off with a little Christmas jeer. Who'd like to go first?"

Hands shoot up, and the jokes begin.

"Little Timmy leaves a note for Santa that reads: if you leave a brand new bike under the tree, I'll give you the antidote for the poison you just ate in that cookie…"

"I figure that that holidays are truly a magical time because it makes all my money disappear…"

"I keep telling my grandkids that Christmas is a time for helping others in need, and that I really need help shoveling my front walk…"

The jokes continue as Lincoln looks at their motley group with fondness, remembering that fateful day several years ago when Lincoln and his friend Oriole Hooper were recovering after a Christmas shopping marathon with their wives…in July. They were at the Avalon Grill, commiserating over chicken fried steak and apple pie. At the table next to them, four men in their eighties had chuckled. The men were all residents of Harmony Homes and knew this problem all too well.

"Welcome to the Club," one of them had said. The elderly men had exchanged a look, then after a silent exchange waved for Lincoln and Oriole to join them.

The leader of the group, Willis Stampend, then 86, took to sneaking a few of them out once a month. It wasn't a big deal, because most Harmony Homes residents could come and go as they pleased so long as they signed themselves in and out, but Willis resented telling anybody where he was going. So these little outings were a rebellion of sorts and gave the men a sense of freedom. They never went far even though Alvin Isaacs once proposed a trip to San Diego, which involved hitch hiking and something to do with a guy named Craig and a list he kept. The men just wanted to be out every now and then, and formed the Bah Humbug Club as a way to justify their outings. The one thing that bonded them together was their distaste for how people these days seemed to focus on all the wrong things, especially during the holidays.

But then the idea took off. Husbands tired of the hype and commercialism, of the obnoxiously cheery decorations shouting at them in stores that began while the heat of the summer is still on. Word spread, and now there's almost forty men in the group.

"It's too much!" Oriole had said that day, his mouth full of mashed potatoes and gravy. His wife, Hermina, had stuck him in a Santa's outfit the Christmas prior for a church function. Two kids peed on his lap and one pulled down his beard. Another demanded to know why he didn't get a pony last year.

"My wife's putting me in the poor house," Dick Whatley tells the group now. "I was cleaning out the attic the other week when I found a pile of gifts, already wrapped."

The gifts had been hidden behind the steamer trunks that held old suits and his wife's wedding dress. When he brought the gifts down to show Ann Marie, she couldn't remember when she'd put them up there. So they'd opened the presents, one by one, Ann Marie delighted by each one, Dick horrified as he realized what this meant. Apparently she had a habit of purchasing presents throughout the year for friends, family, and neighbors, even Dick's co-workers. Whenever she'd forgotten where she'd put them, she'd gone out and shopped some more.

"She raided our vacation fund! Pretended not to know a thing about it. And there we were, sitting around the table, surrounded by the evidence, mind you, and she's telling *me* to relax. I told her the only way that would happen is if we cut up her credit cards!"

"I'm getting a rash from this sweater I got last Christmas," Henry Welch complains, scratching at his neck. "But Helen says I have to wear it. She gives me one every year. One year it, er, accidentally caught fire, another year the cat somehow tore it up." The guilty look on his face is a dead giveaway, and everyone laughs. "So now she locks it up as soon as Christmas is over and takes it out after Thanksgiving. I think she replaces the batteries every night, too." He flicks a button on the cuff of one sleeve and suddenly a string of Christmas lights woven into the sweater begin to blink. "I really hope I don't get electrocuted. And...hold on..." Henry lifts the other cuff and presses another button. Suddenly the tinny sound of "Rudolph the Red-Nosed Reindeer" can be heard coming from somewhere beneath Henry's armpits. He sighs and the rest of the gang pretends to roll their eyes but really can't stop laughing.

"You all have it good," Chester Flores informs the group. "I gain twenty pounds every holiday. All the sweets, you know. Maria's always baking, and it's rough. It takes me eleven months to lose it, and then one month to put it back on. It gets harder every year and my doctor is threatening me with medication if I don't get it under control."

"You should hear my grandkids," Roscoe Copeland says. "It gets worse every year. 'I want this,' 'Gimmee that.' They don't know the value of the dollar, and then they tear through the gifts and get bored a second later. If they don't like the gift, they complain. The older ones even ask if there's a gift receipt so they can return it! I had one grandkid ask for cash straight out. I don't even think they care if I show up or not."

"I want to know what happened to 'peace on earth,

good will to men,'" Russell Rogers says. "Two people stole my parking spot today. I had to drop my wife off and circle the block several times before I found another spot!"

Lincoln taps his pencil on a pad of paper. "So I think we're all in agreement that it seems to be getting worse, not better. People no longer remember what the holidays are all about. And what do we say to that?"

"Bah humbug!" comes the dutifully chorus, and then a round of applause.

"Bah humbug is right," Lincoln says. "We know that this time of year is more than just presents and bright lights and fifty-dollar Christmas trees, right?"

"I wish my tree had cost fifty dollars," Greg Doyle mutters. "Our entry way has twelve foot ceilings and Carole spent well over a hundred dollars on a ten-foot noble fir. She insists that the smaller ones make our son Ruben allergic. I almost broke my neck anchoring that thing to the stairway so it wouldn't fall over."

"Bah humbug!" intones the group.

Lincoln continues to read down his list. "Do we all agree that the spirit of Christmas has been lost, and that people are reluctant to give, much less help, their fellow man in need?"

"Yes!"

"And that Christmas is a time for people to gather with their loved ones, a time for forgiveness and reconciliation of past wounds?"

"Yes!"

Lincoln removes his glasses and gives them a quick clean with the cuff of his shirt. "All right then. Henry, will you give the treasurer's report?"

Henry Welch pulls out a small bank book and manila file. He stands up to make his report. "As of December first, we have over $112,000 in the Bah Humbug fund. We did well in both the bond and stock market, with an average 16% rate of return." He sits back down.

There's a round of applause and someone says, "Sixteen percent? That's a heck of a lot better than I did, this year. Maybe I should let the Bah Humbug Club manage my portfolio, too." There's chortling and laughter.

"Excellent," Lincoln says, nodding. He looks through his notes. "Secretary's next. Luke?"

Luke Cousins stands up. "I've reviewed all the December notes to date. In total over one hundred and seventy-six anonymous random acts of kindness have been documented this holiday season by members of the club, ranging from picking up litter in parking lots to paying overdue fines for library patrons to donating Christmas trees to families in need. Oh, and quite a few of you shoveled your neighbors' walk."

"Hey, we needed the exercise," someone says, and they all laugh.

A hand goes up. "I know we're keeping it anonymous, but I was wondering about the Pick and Save. Was that one of us?"

All heads turn to look at Luke. He shakes his head. "It wasn't on the list."

Lincoln is thoughtful. "I heard about something with the Christmas Bazaar, too. A generous anonymous donation. It seems like we might have a few honorary members of the group." There's a murmuring of approval.

"Not that the wives need to know," Greg reminds the group. "I like that my wife assumes we're just here to fuss and complain. Little does she know that I put a little money aside each paycheck for the Bah Humbug fund."

"My wife knows," Henry says. "She just assumes it goes to beer and food." He pats his shrinking belly and there's more laughter.

"I want to thank all of you for giving so generously this year. Okay, as agreed in our bylaws, fifty percent stays in the fund as principal. Which leaves us with…Henry?"

"Approximately $56,000, give or take."

"Okay, we'll take nominations from the floor. Anyone?"

"I know two families who need a Christmas dinner, tree and presents for the kids…"

"There's a widow on our street whose car just broke down…"

"I'd like us to cover the heating bill for a few nonprofits that seem to be struggling…"

"A few soup kitchens need bodies to help prep and serve on Christmas Day…"

"The houses over on Spring Street are falling into disrepair…"

Luke is taking notes, stopping the suggestions every now and then for more elaboration. Pieces of paper are passed back and forth as ballots are prepared. It seems like a small thing, these anonymous acts that are noticed only by a few and missed by so many, but to the Bah Humbug Club, it's everything.

Lincoln remembers the Christmas that changed everything. It was three years ago. The group had been meeting for five years, and really it was no more than a chance to escape the holiday craziness and blow off some steam to willing, sympathetic ears. But three years ago Willis Stampend, who had been ailing for the past year, had come to the meeting and been quiet throughout. When they finally asked him if everything was all right, he told them the following story.

He had taken his youngest grandchild to the mall in Rockport to see Santa. "You know how much I hate that stuff," he said to them. "But it felt important. I'm ninety one, I can hardly walk with my edema and all, but she wanted to see Santa so we were going to see Santa. The line was long and I felt myself getting tired. Me and this young fellow, about four, who was in line ahead of us. He was fussing and whining and his mother, I swear she didn't look older than twenty and she kept telling him to be quiet. She looked at the end of her rope. Like she really didn't want to there."

Here Willis had sighed and the group leaned in. "So finally we get to the front, and the young fellow goes up, sits on Santa's lap, the elf takes a picture, and the boy launches into a laundry list of things he wants. A new toy truck, airplane, a bike, a rabbit, a swimming pool, that sort of thing. After a minute, his mother marches up there and tells him that's enough. She pulls him off Santa's lap. She's about to leave when Santa asks her what *she'd* like for Christmas.

"Well, this woman just stands there, her mouth hanging open. For a second she looked like a kid, someone who should be hanging out in the mall with her girlfriends or worried about her clothes or hair, not parenting this young boy and, by the looks of it, she wasn't married. Anyway, it takes her a minute but then she says in a whisper, 'I don't believe in Santa.' No one else heard that other than Santa and me, because I'm standing right there. She says this, but she doesn't leave.

"Then Santa says to her, 'You may not believe in me, Patricia, but I believe in you. I believe that you are still the girl most likely to succeed. I believe that you are the one who can achieve anything she sets her mind to. I believe that you are making that boy a fine mother, that you are a fine daughter, neighbor, friend. I believe that you can change whatever situation you are in, for you and your son.' She just listens to him, almost in shock, and I'll be damned if she didn't break down and start crying right then and there. I tell you, when she left there was something different in the way she looked. It was as if a huge burden had been lifted."

There was a stunned silence. Tom Williams had been the first to speak, clearing his throat several times before stammering, "So who...how..."

"I found out later that the guy playing Santa was her old high school principal. Apparently she got pregnant senior year, graduated top of her class but never made it to college. He told me when I spoke with him afterwards—Santa's real name is Hank Polmer and he retired last year from Barrett High. I wrote him a check and asked if he could get it to Patricia and her son. I can't tell you how good that felt." Willis leaned back in his chair and swiped his eyes with the back of his hand. "Well, gentleman, I have to tell you that got me thinking. I'm not much longer on this earth, let's be honest. As it is, I've been luckier than most to be as active as I've been with my cirrhosis, but yesterday the doctor told me I've got liver cancer now. Diagnosis doesn't look good, and I feel different, to tell you the truth. After this holiday, I'm moving back in with the family. We're talking to hospice, too."

Someone coughed, and a few men pulled back, looked away. Someone clapped Willis on the shoulder and one offered a hug. As close as they'd been these past few years, the men were still awkward in the face of death. They can handle the news after the fact, but to be given a deadline by a person still living left them both helpless and uncertain of their own futures.

"So this will most likely be my last meeting with the Bah Humbugs. And I guess I was thinking, after this whole scene at the mall, about what kind of legacy I'm leaving behind. I look back at my life and I gotta tell you, I feel pretty good about it. No regrets. Except this, what we're doing. This high school principal changed someone's life with those few simple words. It's up to her, of course, but he gave her a chance to see things differently, to get a break in whatever script is running through her head and dictating her life. I've enjoyed our camaraderie over the years but I can't help but wonder, can we do more? If we don't like the way the spirit and message of the holiday gets lost, if we think the commercialism has thrown everyone off track, do we want to help make a change instead of gathering and griping? I know I founded this group with that sole intention, but let it be a dying man's wish to ask if it can be different."

The men had looked at one another, and Lincoln had felt his own resolve growing. He had been the first to speak.

"I'm in," he said. "The Bah Humbug Club was your vision, Willis. You knew we all needed a place to vent, to find some common ground. You knew it before we did. I daresay that you might be doing it again. Did you have something specific in mind?"

Willis had nodded and grinned, and Lincoln had just felt it, had known they were on the cusp of something big, important. Willis cleared his throat. "As a matter of fact, I do."

It didn't take them long to come into agreement about keeping their deeds and donations anonymous. They were practical men with a few accountants and a money manager in the mix, so it was easy enough to come up with a framework and formula. They quietly established their fund, and each member agreed to contribute a small amount each month while keeping a list of what they would do for others as the holidays neared.

The one agreement they made was never to reveal who they were or what they were doing. Let the wives and everyone else assume they were merely a bunch of grumpy men who couldn't appreciate the glad tidings of the season.

The first Christmas under their new charter, they bought movie tickets and popcorn vouchers and gave them to families standing in line at the food bank. They saw children jump up and down and weary parents smile at the prospect of a small luxury they wouldn't otherwise be able to afford. Someone wrote in to the *Avalon Gazette* about it and everyone wanted to know who was behind it but of course no one came forward. It was a small gesture but the members of the Bah Humbug Club were hooked. Ideas started flowing in for the following year and they all upped their monthly donations. They discussed how best to invest they money in the Bah Humbug fund during the year to yield maximum returns.

Despite the doctor's diagnosis, Willis Stampend made it the next Christmas, when the members decided to individually find ways to give in addition to giving as a group. They agreed that while they wanted their giving to make an impact, they didn't want to draw any attention to who the donors were—the speculation over the movie tickets had been fun but they risked having their cover blown, too.

"I like that my wife thinks I'm just too lazy to put up lights," one member said. "It's like a competition with her and our neighbor. Who has the better yard, who has the better decorations and lights at Christmas. It's crazy. So last year I anonymously sent them each a gift certificate for a spa day in Rockport—with each other. I know it's a small thing, but they came back friends. Now they figure out how to coordinate their decorations and berate me for not helping, but that's okay. I figure the neighborhood is better for it."

Laughter had run through the group. They quickly saw how acts both big and small rippled into the people and community around them. Anonymous debt payoffs, care packages, gift certificates and cash sent to spouses and families of military service people or left on the windshields of their cars. Airline tickets to see loved ones across the country. In turn, the people they helped found ways to help others, too. The giving, it seemed, never stopped with one person, one act. It began to perpetuate itself throughout the small community of Avalon and, hopefully, beyond.

Willis Stampend passed that following summer, slipping away peacefully after a thirty-six-hour coma, and Lincoln took over as President of the Bah Humbug Club.

This year marks their largest membership ever. And Lincoln knows the group will keep growing—slowing, stealthily—giving the residents of Harmony Homes a chance to leave their mark, if they wish, and for those of them still living in homes of their own a chance to learn a bit of wisdom from those who, as Willis liked to say, "Have walked around the block a few times." The Bah Humbug Club isn't for everyone, and in Harmony Homes it's more of a whispered rumor than proven reality. For Lincoln and the rest of the group, that's just fine. He knows the right people will find them when they're ready.

Room at the Tea Salon

NICOLE GRAY SWEEPS THE LAST of the bread crumbs onto her plate with a happy sigh. It was just what she needed after the long drive, but it's time to get back into her car. She's dreading it, to be honest, because her little hatchback is stuffed to the gills with clothes, books, and other personal belongings. At her garage sale last week, the idea had seemed inspired, even courageous, but now it seems foolish, a whimsy gone bad.

"Oh, I've got that," comes the voice from behind her. Nicole turns in time to see Madeline Davis, owner of Madeline's Tea Salon, approach her with a smile. "You just relax," Madeline says.

"I made a mess," Nicole says, guilty. The scone had been flaky and buttery and Nicole couldn't eat it fast enough. "I can't believe how delicious that was."

"Cranberry orange Amish Friendship Bread scones," Madeline tells her. "With fresh ground nutmeg. It's become a holiday favorite around here. And I like seeing crumbs on a table—I consider them a compliment." She's about to replace Nicole's plate with a new one when Nicole shakes her head.

"Thank you, but I should get the check. I need to get

back on the road." Nicole casts a long look around the room. Inside it's sunny and warm, the kind of place she'd like to curl up with one of her books and spend the day, but outside a snowstorm is raging, the one that made her pull over in the first place. "I have about fourteen hours of driving ahead of me."

"Fourteen hours! Goodness!" Madeline looks so impressed that she pulls up a chair next to Nicole and sits down. "And in this weather! Where are you going in such a rush?"

"Ames, New York. I'm from Ames, Iowa. I know this sounds crazy, but I woke up one morning last month and felt like I was supposed to move east. I didn't know where, but I know it's supposed to be some place small. So I started looking on a map and found Ames, New York. I gave two weeks' notice, packed up last week, and left today. I'm not in a rush, though I guess I'm anxious to see what's going to happen next. I've never lived anywhere else." Nicole feels herself flush.

"From one Ames to another," Madeline murmurs. "Now that's interesting."

"It felt like a safe bet," Nicole confesses. "I'm not quite sure what I'm looking for, to be honest. But so far everything feels right. Well, minus the storm, of course. I hadn't counted on that."

Madeline nods. "I know what that's like," she says, leaning back in her chair. "About things feeling just right. That's what it was like for me when I found Avalon. I was on my way to Chicago and stopped to stretch my legs. Right over there." Madeline points out the window across the street to where Nicole's car is parked and already topped with snow. "I saw the FOR SALE sign and knew this was it. It was where I was supposed to be, where I wanted to be. And then all this—" she gestures to the tea salon around her "—

happened. I couldn't be happier."

Nicole listens, enthralled. Madeline looks to be in her seventies but her blue eyes are bright and she has a youthful look about her. She's peaceful and relaxed despite the fact that she's the owner of this tea salon and serving several customers in addition to Nicole. There's an ease about everything. Nicole feels a longing she hasn't felt before.

It wasn't that Nicole was unhappy in Ames. Listless might be a better word. Aimless in Ames. Nicole had felt unanchored and unmoored despite the fact that her family was there, her friends were there. Even her on-again-off-again boyfriend, Gavin, who didn't understand how she could just pick up and move.

"You're twenty eight," he'd told her, as if she didn't know. They were in their off-again mode, but she had wanted him to know that she was leaving. "And you're taking off for some place you've never even visited? By yourself?"

"It'll be an adventure," she'd said, but she wasn't so sure. "I'm not a kid, Gavin. I want to do more in the world. I want to make a difference."

"So volunteer or whatever," he'd said. "You can do that stuff here."

"I want to try something new. I want to be somewhere new." Nicole was tired of jumping from job to job, her English degree yielding her stints as a proofreader, museum docent, personal assistant, career counselor. It had been in her last job that she had finally decided to take the advice she so freely gave to others. Life not working out? Then change it. So that's what Nicole is doing.

But Gavin had shook his head, scornful. "It's nuts, Nicole."

"It's *not* nuts, Gavin," Nicole had retorted, and in that moment it became clear why their relationship never worked. Everything with Gavin was an argument instead of a discussion. Even when things were going well, his outlook on life was always half empty. And the way he'd said, "It's nuts, Nicole," really meant that he thought *she* was nuts. While Gavin hadn't been part of the reason why she was leaving, he definitely wasn't a reason for her to stay. It was one more piece of evidence that she was moving in the right direction.

This morning when she'd drove out of Ames and later the state, she felt a swell of excitement. She just knew she was heading to some place better.

"Avalon," Nicole says now. She'd seen the sign when she'd driven into town, but since leaving Ames she'd seen a lot of signs. Still, this one stuck out in her mind.

Welcome to Avalon, Pop. 4,243.

"This is home for me," Madeline says simply. "I've lived in quite a few places, and have been fond of several of them, but this is where I've come to hang my hat, so to speak. I'm happy to travel—I have family in Ohio—but there is no place like home, especially if your home is Avalon." A few heads nod around them, overhearing their conversation.

Clara Weber takes a delicate bite of her gingerbread, followed in quick succession by a forkful of upside down cranberry cake. "My husband was born and raised in Avalon. We met in college and came back for Thanksgiving one year. I knew in that moment I wanted to start our family here. We have six grandchildren now, if you can believe that!" Clara reaches for a handful of mini marshmallows and drops them one by one into a steaming mug of cocoa.

Herb "Buster" McMillan takes the hand of the woman seated across from him, a petite brunette named Alicia Rodriguez. "I come and go, but I always return to Avalon. There's just something about this place, you know? Avalon is special."

Alicia adds, "I've only visited a couple of times, but I'm thinking seriously about moving here. Now." She gives Buster a shy smile and he looks surprised, then beams.

"I came in 1976 and haven't looked back since." Boyd Robby takes off his reading glasses as he reaches into his pocket for his wallet. "Well, briefly when Corrine died. I thought it would be too hard to stay at first, but then I realized, there's nowhere else I'd rather be. Corrine loved Avalon."

Again more head nodding.

Madeline turns back to Nicole. "Well, there it is. If you were looking for some place small, Avalon's it. You can't quite have a conversation on your own without other people chiming in, but I wouldn't have it any other way. It's too lonely a life, otherwise." Madeline stands and finished clearing Nicole's table. "I'll get your check."

Too lonely a life. Nicole had never thought about it that way. But even back in Ames, she'd felt that loneliness despite being surrounded by people she cared for and who cared for her.

"Madeline sure does have a way with words," the woman at the next table says. She looks about fifty, her red hair hiding wisps of grey and styled just below her ears. There's a smattering of freckles over her nose, turquoise reading classes perched across the bridge. She looks serious, but mischievous, too, making Nicole think of a pixie.

The woman's table is a four top and there are three people with her, all in their seventies or eighties. One gentleman is hunched over a book, his lips mouthing the words as he reads to himself. He's sitting next to an elegant woman wearing a strand of pearls over her twin set, her grey hair swept into a French chignon. The woman is paging through a book as she makes some notes, her lips moving slightly as she reads. The other gentleman at the table as a couple of newspapers in front of him, *The New York Times* and the *Avalon Gazette*.

The woman with the red hair smiles at Nicole. "Avalon may be a small community, and at times you might have more people in your business than you'd like, but there's always the knowing that the people here have your back. It's a powerful thing, you know?"

"It's funny, though," Nicole confides. "When I lived in Ames, I was surrounded with people I cared about and who cared about me. But I still felt alone. And now that I actually am alone, I don't feel lonely any more. Does that make sense?"

The woman nods and turns her chair to face Nicole. She keeps her voice low as she glances at her tablemates. "Sometimes, then, it's not the people, but you."

"Me?"

"Well, not you specifically, but anyone who's feeling that way isn't always living the life they want to be living. Other people, no matter how much they love you, can't make you happy unless you want to be happy. What kind of work do you do?"

Nicole smiles. "A lot of things—I'm a bit of a jack of all trades. But my last job was as a librarian at the public library."

The woman jerks up, her eyes wide. "No kidding." She scoots her chair closer to Nicole. "Tell me more."

"Well, I love books, so I figured that made the most sense," Nicole explains. "I had been volunteering in a library for a couple of years, and decided to go for my masters degree in library science from Iowa State."

"Good for you."

Nicole give a small smile. "Yes, but the funny thing is that after I got it, I thought I'd be happy, but I wasn't. Technically I was doing what I loved, but it didn't feel like enough."

"Maybe it wasn't," the woman suggests. "What I mean to say is, you said you loved books. Being a librarian isn't necessarily the same thing. Although," the woman casts a quick scan around the tea salon, "we have a wonderful library in Avalon, so I'm certainly not trying to say that being a librarian isn't a wonderful thing."

"Aw, Carla, come on," comes a chuckle from another table. Two men are seated there, one in a white pharmacist's jacket and the other in coveralls. The man in the pharmacist's jacket is sipping a cup of coffee, his ruddy face filled with mirth. "Give the girl full disclosure."

The woman—Carla Pike—gives him a look. "Mind you own business, Clyde."

"Carla here is the owner of the Book Nook, our new and used bookstore," Clyde tells Nicole. "She's always trying to grab any new book lovers to come work for her instead of the library."

"It is not an either or situation," Carla says with a disgusted snort. She turns back to Nicole. "Ignore him. That's Clyde Thomas, our local pharmacist. He'll fill your prescription and your ear with a load of nonsense."

"Nonsense?" Clyde snorts. He waggles a finger at Carla. "I happen to know that Lori Blair has gone full-time with the *Gazette* and Nathan quit to go back to UI to finish his degree. And with the holiday rush and all, you are probably in desperate need of some help."

"Oh, Carla, why didn't you tell us?" exclaims the older woman at her table. "We're taking up your precious time, especially during this holiday season. I know how important these holiday sales are for a business."

"It's all right, Ella," Carla says, shooting Clyde a look. "Things have been slow, even with the holidays, but don't worry about it." Her tablemates are looking at her now, their faces full of concern. Carla sighs and throws up her hands. "*It's all right, everyone.* Look, it's just a rough patch, and I'll get through it. You know I always do."

Clyde sips his coffee. "You see, unlike a library which has some public funding—"

"Not much," Carla interjects. "Bernice has to work just as hard as I do to manage her budget at the Avalon Library."

"—Carla here is on her own," Clyde continues. "All her efforts come out of her own pocket. She does a lot of outreach reading programs in the community, like at the elementary and high school—"

"She volunteers at the library, too…" someone chimes in.

"And she reads to us at Harmony Homes, a senior residential facility just on the edge of town. She also takes several of us out each week, like now, and I treasure this time," Ella says. Her voice is full of gratitude. "It doesn't feel like a field trip or excursion—it just feels like life." The two men at their table nod.

"*And* she works with small business owners when they're first starting out." Clyde waves his coffee mug in the direction of his friend. "Right, Alfie?"

"I couldn't have done it without you, Carla," Alfie says. He hands Nicole a business card that reads ALFIE'S AUTOMOTIVE, *From Tune-Ups To Engine Overhauls, We Do It All.* "I offered to give her free oil changes for life, but she refuses."

"She's always sponsoring reading and writing contests," Clyde continues, enjoying Carla's discomfort. "And donating books. And her time. And—"

"Okay, everyone. *Enough.*" Carla looks put out but Nicole can tell she's a little pleased, too. "I swear, you'd think I haven't been in business on my own for fifteen years already." She shakes her head.

"Well, it's no secret that libraries and bookstores are struggling these days," Madeline says, joining in on the conversation as she wipes down a vacated table. "And what you've done, Carla, is quite remarkable." To Nicole, Madeline says, "It's a shame you have to leave. It's worth a visit to the Book Nook if you can. It's right around the corner."

"Though by the looks of things, it'll be iffy if anyone pays me a visit today," Carla says, nodding to the window. "I think, my friends, that I'd better get you all back to Harmony Homes." Her voice is light but there's a hint of wary concern.

Nicole turns to look outside and sees that the weather has ratcheted up several knots. The wind is fierce, the snow spinning and eddying, obscuring their view beyond a few feet of the window.

"That goes for me, too," Clyde says, wiping his mouth. "Don't want anyone to go without their meds, especially if we end up snowed in."

Snowed in? Nicole looks at her watch. It's already half past eight, and she still has three states and 878 miles to go.

Carla is helping the Harmony Homes residents into their coats, and Nicole jumps up to give a hand. She holds up a heavy wool coat as the taller man slips into it, then hands him his hat and scarf.

"Thank you," the man says with a smile. "By any chance was that your car parked outside across the street? Iowa plates? Filled to the brim with boxes and books?"

Nicole nods, embarrassed. "I couldn't bear to leave them behind," she says. "That's pretty much all I've got with me. My clothes and my books. It's kind of sad."

"Not at all," the man says. "On the contrary, it shows you have a fine mind. And it's fitting that you should meet Carla." He pauses, studying Nicole for a moment, before scooping up his newspapers and tucking them under his arm. He taps at a multicolored weather map. "Looks like we might be in for a rough couple of days. Not just here, but across the country. Heavy snowstorms. I wouldn't advise being on the roads, if you can avoid it." There's a flicker of lights as the electricity surges.

"And with that, it is officially time to go," Carla interjects, ushering them out the door. She turns to give Nicole a small wave. "I'd love to talk books with you some more if you end up staying in town. I'll be at the shop regardless of the weather—my house is in the back of the store—and it's within walking distance to Madeline's. You're welcome to come by any time."

"Thank you," Nicole says.

The rest of the tea salon patrons are quick to pay their bill and head on their way. Nicole, however, is slow to gather her things. Connie Colls, the young tea salon manager with spiky black hair and an apron tied around her waist, begins to clear the tables.

What should Nicole do? It's not supposed to go like this. Nicole was supposed to leave Ames for Ames, end of story. No bad weather, no detours, no chatting in tea salons. Now her whole schedule is off and she doesn't have a place to stay to ride out the storm. As anxious as she is to start her new life, it's clear she's not going anywhere anytime soon.

"Excuse me," Nicole says. "But do you happen to know of any places where I could stay around here?"

Connie stops to think. "Gosh, I'm not sure. We have a list out front of a couple of B&B's but I know they're full up with the holidays. You could call them to see if they have any cancellations. Otherwise you'd have to go towards Barrett or Laquin to find a motel." She gives Nicole an apologetic look, glancing outside at the worsening storm.

Madeline steps out of the kitchen, drying a large serving

dish with a tea towel. "I have an odd invitation for you," she says. "If you'd like, you are welcome to stay here at the salon until this all blows over. It's just me and Connie and we have plenty of room. This building used to be a B&B, as a matter of fact, so you can have your own room and bath."

Connie gives an enthusiastic nod. "That's a great idea," she says. "What do you say?"

"I don't know," Nicole says, feeling both relief and guilt. "I mean, I don't want to impose. If I could pay you something..."

"Nonsense," Madeline says. "Stay as our guest. I wouldn't feel right if you headed out in this weather. Connie and I have quite a bit of cooking to do today, so we won't be much for entertaining, but the Book Nook is right around the corner if you're looking for something new to read. I'm sure Carla would appreciate the company if you wanted to walk over and say hi once you're settled in."

"I can help you bring in whatever you need from your car," Connie offers.

Nicole feels something shifting into place. She doesn't know what it is just yet, but she's willing to find out. "Okay," she says. "Thank you."

"Over here we have local history, American history, world history," Carla is saying. She points to a row of bookshelves. "Self help, how to, cooking, arts and crafts. Over there, literature and fiction, mysteries, memoir, biographies. The second floor is the children and young adult section. Everything else is pretty self-explanatory—I hope so, at least. Anyway, feel free to take a look around."

Nicole peers into the back of the shop where a fireplace is lit up with a crackling fire. There are lots of plush sitting chairs, a round oak table top with six antique ladderback chairs. Framed prints are on the wall, quotes and silhouettes of famous authors. Bouquets of silk flowers dot the shelves here and there, offering an unexpected burst of color. Knickknacks are tucked into any empty space—a miniature globe, a bird cage, an old large format camera, a Rubik's cube, small baskets filled with marbles or other odds and ends. There are bookends in the shape of animals and seashells and letters of the alphabet. There's a whole section for used books, too, spilling off the shelves onto stacks lining one entire wall.

"I've been needing to clean house for a while," Carla says. "But it's my own version of shabby chic—the overflow of books adds to the ambiance, I think. Plus it gives me more choices when I change up the selection at Harmony Homes." She hands Nicole a large basket. "Do me a favor and fill this up with any used books you think they might like. There's a whole section of large print and audio over there, too. You've never seen so many happy people when I bring in new books, let me tell you. I feel like a regular Santa Claus."

"So it's just you here?" Nicole asks.

Carla nods as she pushes aside stacks of bills and papers. "I was a voracious reader when I was a kid, so this is heaven for me. But I'd be lying if I said it was easy. I'm not one to begrudge the big bookstores or the advent of digital books, but it's putting a serious dent in my business, that's for sure. I volunteer at the Avalon Public Library, too, and it's not any easier for Bernice to get new patrons into the library. It's just too easy nowadays for people to stay home and order something to be shipped to their door or download it on the spot. The art of browsing through shelves and coming upon an unexpected author or book is over, it seems." Carla shakes her head.

"That's my favorite part," Nicole says. "The weight of the book in your hand. The feel of the book. The smell of the book."

"I agree. There's something magical about it. Books are waiting to be discovered by new readers all of the time." Carla sighs.

"I was intrigued by all your community outreach efforts," Nicole tells her. She's walking the aisles, slipping her selections into the basket.

"You should see what I've done over at Harmony Homes," Carla chuckles. "They gave me a corner to start with but each week I expand our area by a few inches, hoping they don't notice. It's my intention to convert that entire rec room into a reading room. I also host a book club for some of the more avid readers though it's never more than five or six people."

"How are you able to do everything? The store, your community work…it seems like it would take up a lot of your time."

"It takes up all of my time," Carla tells her. "I live and breathe this store, these books." She looks around the store. "I would be happy even if I didn't have a single customer in here. That's part of the fun, of course, helping people find a book that will delight them, or educate them, or inspire them. But I knew from the get go that I was doing this for me, because I love it. I don't think I would have weathered the more difficult times if I hadn't been as passionate about it. They always say you work harder when a business is your own, and while that's true, I think the real difference is that you don't give up as easily. I'm motivated to do whatever it takes to make this work."

The door swings open and a few customers come in. "Still open?" asks one.

"Always open," Carla replies, giving Nicole a wink. "Go

roam, Nicole. In general I don't allow beverages or food in the store for obvious reasons, but there's a small kitchenette in the back that you're welcome to for tea or coffee. Find a book and make yourself at home."

"Whew," Carla says, turning the sign on the door from OPEN to CLOSED. "I am done for the day. It was a good day, considering…" Her voice trails off and she shakes her head. "So how are you doing?" Carla grins when she sees the basket by Nicole's chair is full. "Oh, I like your selections. Couldn't have done better myself."

"What time is it?" Nicole asks. She looks outside and sees that it's dusk.

"Almost six," Carla says. "That mad rush in the end kept me open an extra forty five minutes, not that I'm complaining." She falls into the overstuffed armchair across from Nicole, lets her reading glasses dangle from their chain. "Madeline called and invited me to join you all for dinner. Something about chicken pot pies and tomato soup, plus a rhubarb crumble for dessert."

"Oh, that sounds wonderful," Nicole says. She puts down the leather-bound copy of *Treasure Island* she was reading and gives a stretch.

Carla's eyes widen as she looks around the room. "Hey, something seems different in here," she says. "What were you up to?"

"I straightened up a bit," Nicole confesses, reddening. "Some of the books were out of order but I didn't want people to not find what they were looking for. I also dusted and wiped down some of the mustier areas. I brought the bookends in tight and all the spines up to the edge to create a more uniform look. I also rotated this carpet because it looked like it was getting pretty worn in a few places. I hope that's okay."

"Okay? This place looks amazing!" Carla shakes her head in wonderment.

"I only got through the fiction shelves," Nicole says. "Before I found this and started reading." She holds up the book. "Robert Louis Stevenson is one of my favorite authors. I love this leather-bound edition. The slip case is gorgeous."

"Not to mention the gilded edges and printed endpapers," Carla says, nodding. "It's one of my favorites, too." She looks around the room again. "Wow."

Nicole blushes. "It was already is good shape," she begins.

"Oh, stop. We both know that's not the case," Carla says. She hesitates for a moment and then sighs. "I'll admit I've let a few things fall by the wayside. I'll admit, too, that I'm just barely keeping my head above the water. And, while I'm at it, the real reason Lori and Nathan are gone is because I told them a few months back that I'd have to let them go. I didn't want to make a big fuss with everyone earlier but I think I'm closing shop. For good. I'm waiting until after the holidays to tell people."

Nicole frowns. "But you just had a bunch of customers...and all the work you're doing at Harmony Homes..."

Carla shakes her head. "It's not enough. I'll always do what I can for Harmony Homes, and who knows, maybe this will free me up to do more. But as a business, I've been suffering. Have been for a while. It's a tough time for bookstores, especially small ones like mine. I don't have the inventory like the online stores, I can't offer the same discounts. I spoke with a business broker earlier this year and he didn't think I'd have much luck selling it because it's clear the numbers don't work. My savings are gone and I don't have any working capital left. I can't get out of the red." Carla is glum.

"I'm so sorry," Nicole says.

"Me too." Carla gives a sad chuckle. "But it's nice to get it off my chest. Thank goodness you're passing through town. I don't want anyone in Avalon knowing my situation, because they'll all just come in and buy something out of sympathy, and I don't want that. I want the Book Nook to stand on its own, you know?"

"But all local businesses rely on the patronage and support of the community," Nicole says. "I mean, that's how local businesses thrive. They're not sympathy buys, it's a willingness to support the retailers in the community. An independent bookstore relies on the community—it's there *for* the community."

The look on Carla's face is dark. "Well, why haven't they come sooner? Everyone's great when we're talking about books and chatting about how wonderful they think the Book Nook is, but when it's time to purchase a book, they go online or to one of the bigger bookstores in the city. I hate to be frustrated, because they're all good people here, but my bookstore is about to go under."

"You have to give them a chance," Nicole says. "You can't just spring it on them that you're closing your doors. You need to give them an opportunity to help. You said yourself that Avalon is a place where people have your back. And maybe at the same time you could think about changing the way you do things a bit. Figure out new ways to get people to buy books or host events. Not the stuff people have done for years, but something different, innovative. Bookstores are going under, it's true, but many are thriving, too. Why can't yours be one of them?"

"Nicole, I wish I'd gotten a shot of your enthusiasm a

year ago. Now, I'm afraid, it's too late. I have at most sixty days by which time I will also be as broke as broke can be." Carla stands up and offers to help pull Nicole out of her chair. "Come on, let's go eat. Thank you, though. I appreciate you being a willing ear. I've missed having someone else here. And keep the book. Something to remember me by."

They walk back to Madeline's, silent. As they near the tea salon, they're surprised to see cars pulled into the driveway and lined up along the street.

"What's going on?" Carla asks as they pull open the front door. Inside, it's warm and packed with people.

"A few blocks lost electricity," someone tells them. "Electric company can't get out until the morning, so Madeline invited us over for dinner."

"And anyone who needs a warm place to stay is welcome to take up residency in any of the extra rooms or sitting areas," Madeline says, coming out with a large platter of green beans. "I thought I'd cook up what I can in case we lose electricity, too, though I hope not."

"Someone can stay with me," Nicole says. "There's a queen bed and I can sleep on the sofa in the room."

"The Bentley sisters might take you up on that," Madeline says, nodding to two elderly women standing in the corner, looking worried. "I'll let them know."

"There's room at the store," Carla volunteers. "And the small apartment upstairs used to hold my inventory but it's pretty much cleaned out. We can fit a few people up there, and there's a private bath and kitchen, too."

"I've called around and quite a few neighbors have offered their guest rooms to anyone who needs one," Connie says. "I think we got every one—if not, we'll figure it out after dinner."

They go around the room, each person taking a moment

to thank Madeline for the meal and expressing their gratitude for having found a warm place to stay. Nicole feels her spirits buoy, higher than they've ever been in months. As they sit down and pick up their forks, there's laughter, the sound of friendship. She hasn't even been in Avalon a day and already she feels at home.

During dessert Carla taps the side of her water glass with a spoon. Nicole feels a flash of dread, knowing what Carla's about to do. "Carla," she begins.

Carla looks at her and smiles. "It's okay," she says. "If it weren't for you I wouldn't have the guts to do this now." She clears her throat. "Everyone, I want to share with you something I've been keeping a secret for a while. I'm sorry to say that the Book Nook is closing—for good. I'll have a little less than two months in the new year so if there's anything special you're looking for, come in after the holidays."

There's a stunned silence.

"What in tarnation are you talking about, Carla?" Clyde Thomas demands. "Why didn't you say anything this morning?"

"Why didn't I say anything all year?" Carla asks. "I guess I thought things might turn around, or maybe I was just putting off the inevitable. Anyway, what difference does it make now, Clyde?"

"It makes a heck of a lot of difference," Clyde says. He turns to his wife. "Hazel loves the Book Nook, Carla. Me, too."

"Come on, Clyde," Carla chides. "We both know you don't read anything other than those pharmaceutical journals and the sports page."

Clyde puts his hands up. "Well, that might be true, but when the grandkids are in town, you know that's where we go. I like that we can choose a book to read together when they're with us, and then they get to take it back home with them."

"It's become a ritual," Hazel Thomas agrees. "And just where am I supposed to get the latest romances now?"

"Carla, the bookstore can't close." Amanda Bentley is speaking now. "You're the only place willing to do all those special orders for us." She explains to everyone else, "Ticia is a Maeve Binchy fan. Loves all her books and tries to get signed editions. I'm more of a mystery reader myself and Carla has helped me find some real classics."

"Surely something can be done," Connie says, a despondent look on her face. She glances at Madeline, worried.

"Is there anything we can do to help?" Madeline asks.

"No, no. I've tried every trick in the book. I've exhausted all my possibilities." Carla's eyes are damp and she dabs the corners with a napkin.

"Well, not all," Nicole says. "I mean, it's not over until it's over, right? What about selling it?"

"It's over," Carla says with finality. "I told you that I spoke with a business broker who said that he didn't think it would sell. It doesn't make any money and every bookstore in the country is going through the same thing. Not a lot of flush buyers out there wanting to take a chance on a floundering business." She gives a small smile. "Unless you're interested, Nicole. The Book Nook could use an injection of your smarts."

"I am interested," Nicole says, and there's a collective gasp.

"But how?" Carla asks, her face lit up in hope. "You're young. You probably don't have enough money. I mean, no offense, Nicole."

"No, you're right." There's a confused murmuring. Nicole quickly adds, "It's true, I don't have enough money to buy a business. I do, however, have enough money to buy part of a business."

Carla looks confused. "What do you mean?"

"I think you should offer shares of the Book Nook, like a cooperative. That way people who want to help can, and because they'll be part owners, so to speak, and we'll all be much more invested in the Book Nook's success. You wouldn't have to figure out how to make the Book Nook successful on your own, because everyone would contribute ideas and support. I'm sure there are successful models out there, Carla. We could call those bookstores and learn more."

"I don't know," Carla says. "No matter how you slice it, bookstores aren't the best financial investment."

"People wouldn't be doing this just for financial gain," Nicole says. "They would be doing it because they want a bookstore as amazing as the Book Nook in their community. What I like about the cooperative idea is that you can have shares priced so that almost anybody could be a part of it, if they want. It's a cash injection, yes, but you would also have the resources of the group available to you when it came to planning or marketing. I'm sure there are lawyers, or financial people, or people with marketing skills who you could call on for help, and you won't feel guilty or obligated because it's theirs, too."

"I like the idea of owning part of something," Claribel Apple declares.

"Me, too," Clyde Thomas says.

"We would want to be a part of this," Ticia Bentley says. "Right, Amanda?"

"Absolutely," Amanda says. "You can count on us to contribute in a significant way, Carla."

"Please include me," Madeline says. "If I hadn't opened a tea salon, a bookstore would have been the next best thing." She smiles.

"I'm in."

"So am I."

"I know all the ladies in my book club would want to buy shares," Maureen Nyer says. "Or we could pool our money together to make it happen. When will you know how much each share will be?"

Carla is speechless. She turns to Nicole, a stunned look on her face. "Is this really happening?" she asks in disbelief.

Nicole just grins. She knows with an odd certainty that the Book Nook will not only survive, but flourish. She also knows, to echo the words Madeline spoke earlier, that she has found a place to hang her hat. That she won't need to drive any further than where she is right now. That she now has a good idea about what she'll be doing with her life, at least for now. Beyond that, she has no idea, but the one thing Nicole knows, she won't be alone. She joins the small crowd gathered around Carla, and leans to give her new friend a hug.

Secret Santa

MARY MCLEAN HANGS UP the phone, a look of dread on her face. "Bad news," she tells Daryl, the other certified nurse aide who is sharing the evening shift with her.

Daryl looks up from a partially completed crossword puzzle. "These are hard," he says, tapping his pen against the paper. "I've never been able to finish one of these. The theme is 'Where's Santa?' and twenty across is a long one. What's a 1966 Johnny Rivers hit?"

"I have no idea," Mary says. "I don't even know who Johnny Rivers is." She squints at the newspaper. "It looks like you filled out quite a bit of the crossword, though."

"Nah, it wasn't me. I found it like this in the rec room." Daryl sighs and pushes the paper away. "So what's the bad news?"

"The person I found to play Santa Claus can't make it," Mary says. "He has the flu and can't find anyone else to replace him." She looks at the clock which reads 5:00 p.m. Outside darkness has already fallen. "And all the families are about to arrive."

Daryl makes a face. "Hey, sorry about that. I know you worked hard trying to find someone."

Mary sighs. "I know. They charge so much, too. It'll be

impossible to find someone who can replace him at such late notice. Unless…" She gives Daryl a hopeful look.

"What? No. That's not in my job description. Plus anyone looking at me knows it's me. Not a lot of 6'4" Santas running around here." Daryl reaches for the paper again. "How about this: forty-one across says 'Stop right there!' It's six letters, beginning with the letter F."

"Freeze," Mary says, picking up a phone book.

"Freeze…wait, that's right! Cool." Daryl writes it in. "Wow, I'm doing a *New York Times* crossword puzzle." A second later he pushes the puzzle away again. "Boy, this place is rubbing off on me. Next thing you know I'll be wanting all my food pureed, too."

"That's not nice," Mary says. "We all get old someday, Daryl."

"Yeah, but I'm twenty eight and you're, what, twenty five, twenty six? It's not our time yet, thank God. Hey, Mr. Peterson, what are you doing up and about?" Daryl jumps up from behind the nurse's desk, giving Mary a surprised look.

"What does it look like I'm doing? I'm going for a stroll." Clark Peterson wheels by them, his chin lifted in proud defiance.

They watch him roll down the hall in his wheelchair. "How the heck did he get out of his bed on his own?" Daryl asks, scratching his head.

"Maybe you should have asked," Mary says, giggling. "I think he's sweet on Alice Edwidge, now that she's back. Sometimes it takes a crisis to bring people together."

"Ol' Elden Burns isn't going to like that," Daryl says with a chuckle. "He and Alice seem like they're an item. Mr. Peterson's got some catching up to do." He picks up the crossword again.

"Well, maybe he's up for the challenge of going after the

girl he loves. It's not his time yet either, it seems." She gives Daryl an amused smile, and then her face crumples again. "But what should we do about Santa?"

"No one knew he was coming tonight," Daryl points out. "You scheduled that on your own, Mary, so no harm done. We'll just keep the music going and pass out candy canes and greet the families when they come in for Christmas dinner and caroling. No biggie." The Avalon Octaves have offered to come in to sing while the residents and their visiting families are eating turkey and ham. For Daryl, that seems like plenty of Christmas cheer.

"But I wanted to surprise everyone," Mary insists. "The Christmas party was a bit of a letdown with Mrs. Edwidge getting hurt…"

"Hold up," Daryl says, interrupting her. He knows she worked hard to make the Christmas party special for the residents, just like she does with everything at Harmony Homes. He hates to spoil it for her, but he's worked here longer than her and knows that this place can burn you out if you're not careful. He's survived the years by keeping himself one step removed and not getting emotionally involved with the residents, even though he does have a few favorites, like Lottie Rush and Eloi Doyle. "That party was a success—these things happen. It's sad, but true. You've done more than anybody else for these people since I've worked here, Mary."

"These aren't just 'people,' Daryl," Mary says, her voice vehement. "Not to me. These people are family as far as I'm concerned." She's blinking back tears and starts flipping through the phone book, tearing a few of the tissue-thin pages in her haste.

Daryl feels bad, remembering the rumor that Mary had lost her parents in a fire when she was young. She'd been raised by her grandparents who had passed away right around the time she graduated from high school. Well, that made sense if you thought about it. Daryl's here because the job's easy, has pretty good benefits and free meals. Plus it's less than ten minutes from his house which is good for a guy who likes to roll out of bed and go. But Mary's here because these people seem to mean something to her, or remind her of people she used to love.

"Hey, I'm sorry," he says, his voice softening. He sighs, resigned. "And if you want me to dress up like Santa, I will. I'll look ridiculous, but whatever."

"Really?" Mary's face brightens and Daryl can't help grinning.

"Yeah, why not?" Everyone at Harmony Homes will get a kick out of it, and at least none of his friends will see him. They'd never let him live it down. Being a nurse is bad enough—some of his friends had gone on to play ball for college, one even went pro for the Chicago Steam. Daryl had been a guy with a future, a big future, and even Notre Dame was hot to recruit him. But then a stupid pickup basketball game the summer before his senior year in high school left him with a torn Achilles tendon. Game over.

"I think you'll make a wonderful Santa Claus," Mary says, eyes shining, and Daryl squirms with embarrassment. He used to think it was all an act, her earnestness and cheerfulness, but he knows now it's just the way she is. He doesn't know anyone else quite like her. He clears his throat and pretends to look down at the crossword again.

"I wonder if the costume will fit though." Mary's brows furrow as she takes him in, and he blushes from behind the paper. "I'd better go check. It's hanging in my locker, I'll go get it." Daryl casually looks up to watch her as she hurries off.

Mary McLean and Daryl Smith—now that's an unlikely pairing if he ever saw one. They're good friends at work, but that's the limit of their friendship.

Still, it's funny—Mary seems to be the only person he knows that accepts him just as he is. She doesn't know about his friends or family, about his own personal life that he's always made a point of keeping to himself because he doesn't want sympathy. Like his father leaving them when Daryl was just a baby, driving off in the only car they owned. About a sister who passed at the age of six from acute lymphocytic leukemia. Mary doesn't know about how he almost flunked out his senior year, angry and unable to concentrate. Daryl barely graduated high school, but he did. For a couple of years he did nothing, a few odd jobs here and there, and he slept. A lot.

Then one night, he awoke and had the distinct feeling that he was not alone in the room. Scared isn't the right word—it was more like he was suddenly aware. Something was there with him, he was certain of it. And he knew something was about to happen.

But nothing did. He sat there in his bed, in the dark, listening to the quiet night. He still lived at home, knew his mother was fast asleep so she could wake up by 5:30 a.m. to get breakfast on the table for him and then head off to work as a public safety dispatcher. She would tell him about some of the calls she received. His mother was the first point of contact for people calling in on 9-1-1 emergency lines. Some of the stories were funny, some were sad, some were downright scary. He never thought about it until that moment, but it was incredible what she did. To keep calm in the face of a crisis, sometimes a life or death crisis, and to get people the help they needed. Just like what she'd been doing for Daryl all these years.

Even though it was a moonless night, Daryl saw the catalog on his desk. How long it had been there, he had no idea, but it was a course catalog for community college almost an hour and a half away. He got up from the bed, turned on his desk lamp, and sat down. He stayed up the rest of the night, and then surprised his mother by having breakfast on the table for her by the time she woke up.

Later, his mother would deny ever having put it that catalog, even putting up a mild protest when he got accepted, suggesting that he choose a school closer to Avalon so he could save his money and continue to live at home. But no, it was done and Daryl knew it was time.

So he went on to Illinois Valley Community College, even played basketball for them. He got his CNA certification, and now he's been thinking about taking some online classes to get his associate's degree and maybe become a registered nurse. It's an option, anyway, and better than the ones his friends are faced with. Not everyone gets to play ball for a living.

No, Mary doesn't know any of that, but he gets the feeling that it wouldn't make a difference either way. She seems to like him just as he is, and that's saying a lot. She's a good person with a good heart. Even on the days when he doesn't feel like coming to work, the minute he sees her he feels like his day just got a whole lot brighter.

Daryl looks through a few charts, makes a note of the time. A few residents pass by and he chats with them, reminding them about Christmas dinner, caroling, and a holiday bingo Mary has set up for the evening. In a few minutes he'll do his rounds.

"Daryl!" Mary's voice makes him jerk up his head. She's rushing towards him, a frantic look on her face. "The Santa costume. It's gone!"

"Gone?"

"It wasn't in my locker and I've had it there all week!"

"You think somebody stole it?"

"Maybe, but…" Mary lowers her voice. "My locker was

still locked. And they didn't take my purse or anything else."

"It must be those tricky elves..."

She swats him. "Daryl, I'm serious." But a small smile plays on her lips.

A middle-aged woman with two children are wandering the halls, a lost look on their face. Daryl stands up and walks over.

"Can I help you?" he asks.

The woman bites her lip, still looking around. "My father...I can't find him. He's not in his room. His bed's made...well, it's always made so I'm not sure that's saying much...but there isn't a sign of him anywhere. Every time I've come before—" The woman drops her head in guilt. "Well, it's been a while but he usually has a cup of coffee and his crossword puzzle out. I didn't see either on his table."

Daryl goes back to the nurse's station and holds up the paper. "This it, by chance?"

The woman studies it. "Yes, that's his handwriting! Well, except for that word there."

Daryl reddens. "That was me. It was the only one I got."

The woman nods, studying the paper. "Twenty across is *Secret Agent Man*. Thirty five across is 'ivey.' And forty six down is 'arte' with an 'e'."

Daryl fills in the squares. "Wow, you're good. Like father, like daughter, right? Who'd you say your dad was again?"

"Melvin. Melvin O'Malley. I...I told him that it didn't look like we'd be around for the holidays, because I thought we would be in L.A., but they cancelled our flight on account of the weather. And the kids want to see him." She brings her two children close to her, a boy and a girl. The kids look bored. The woman, on the other hand, is a different story altogether.

Mary is beaming. "He'll be so glad you're here to see him," she says to them. "And I hope you'll be able to stay for dinner. We'll be singing Christmas carols and we have some other activities planned. Several women in town brought over a selection of baked goods for dessert, too." She holds out a basket of candy canes for the kids, who each take one.

The woman looks uncomfortable, and Daryl distracts them all by picking up Melvin's file. "Your name?" he asks.

"Barbara Lowe. Well, Barbara O'Malley Lowe. And this is Ty and Jessica, his grandkids."

It checks out in the file. Daryl catches Mary's eye. "I'll check his room and then the common room. You can keep looking around for, you know, the suit."

Mary gives him a thumbs up and another earnest smile. Daryl tries not to look flustered as he motions for Barbara and the kids to follow him. "I'm sure he's around here somewhere, though he's been out and about lately. He has full privileges, which means he can go into town if he wants. We can check at the front if he signed out."

"How?"

"We have a shuttle but sometimes he calls a cab. There are also a few volunteers that take the residents out every now and then. It's good for them to see people outside of Harmony Homes."

Barbara nods, swallowing. Daryl wants to kick himself— he hadn't meant to make her feel bad. But who's she kidding? She's vaguely familiar to Daryl, which means she doesn't come by much. Melvin's a grumpy guy, that's for sure, and for a long time seemed resentful about being here, not that Daryl blames him. But lately, especially the past couple of weeks since Alice Edwidge's accident, Daryl has noticed a change. A big one.

"Your dad's been in a good mood these past few days,"

Daryl says, trying to make conversation as they walk down the hall. "Must be the Christmas spirit."

"Dad? My dad?" Barbara appears mystified. "That doesn't sound like him."

Daryl gives a shrug. "Maybe not, but that's been the case." He slows as they approach Melvin's room, the door open as they have extended mandatory open door hours during the holidays. When Daryl first started, it seemed like a dumb rule, but now he knows it makes a difference. Many of the residents fall into a depressed stupor during the holidays, but keeping their door open means they can't shut themselves off, that they have to interact on some level, whether they like it or not. And more often than not, those interactions are positive. "Melvin?" he calls. "You in here?"

As expected, there's no answer. Nothing seems amiss, so they head to the common area. It's crowded, with residents and families, but Daryl doesn't see him anywhere. "I'll go check to see if he signed out..." he begins, when the room falls quiet.

"It's Santa!" Jessica exclaims, pointing to the door.

Daryl turns just as a jolly "Ho ho ho!" rings out across the common area. Jessica and Ty and clapping their hands in surprise, and everyone looks delighted. Whoever this guy is, he could pass for the real thing. But who *is* this guy? Already he's making his way around the room, offering a gloved hand in greeting, his other hand holding a strip of large brass bells which he jingles to great effect. He looks familiar, but Daryl can't place him.

"Hey," he's about to say, when he feels a hand on his arm.

"It looks like Santa found us after all," Mary says.

"Is that your suit? Do you know who that is?"

Mary just smiles. "I have my suspicions. It all makes sense now."

Daryl's glad someone knows what's going on because he hasn't a clue. "We can't find Melvin. I'm going to see if he checked out."

Mary shakes her head. "No need. He's here." She smiles again and points to Jessica and Ty who have walked into the center of the common room to get a closer look. Santa turns at that moment and sees the children. He lets out a whoop of surprise and another hearty "Ho ho ho!"

"Son of a gun," Daryl says. Het lets out a whistle. Two weeks ago, he couldn't see Melvin getting into a Santa costume any more than Daryl, but a lot can happen in two weeks. He casts a sidelong glance at Mary who's humming along with the music and thinks, *Yeah, maybe anything is possible.*

Barbara steps forward and Santa leans towards her, whispers something in her ear. The strained tightness of her face disappears, and she smiles, relaxed, and pulls the children to her as Santa ruffles the tops of their heads then continues to make his rounds.

"So I was wondering," Daryl begins, clearing his throat. He looks at Mary and feels his neck redden. "If maybe you want to grab a pizza sometime? After work?" Even as he's asking the question, he knows the whole thing is nuts, but what would really make him crazy is if he didn't even bother asking, if he didn't even try. "I mean, we can go just as friends," he adds quickly. "As co-workers."

Mary doesn't answer right away, but slips her hand in his and gives it a squeeze. "Yes," she breathes after a moment. "I'd like that." There's a squabble breaking out in the far corner of the common room and Mary releases his hand as she hurries to see what's going on. Daryl can still feel the warmth of her palm, can picture the smile tossed over her shoulder as she walks away.

Santa stands before him and Daryl finds himself

unnerved. He looks into sparkling blue eyes and feels a warm clap on his shoulder. There aren't a lot of guys as tall as Daryl but Daryl feels like this guy—Santa? Melvin?—is looking him straight in the eye.

"Under the tree," Santa says, leaning in. "A little something for you. Dinner for two. Take her someplace nice. Forget the pizza."

"What? Who are you, man? You're Melvin, right?"

Santa just smiles, pats him on the arm, and points. Daryl turns and sees a sprig of mistletoe hanging in the doorway, right near where Mary is standing. Santa gives him a wink and just as Daryl is about to protest, to demand an answer *just because*, Santa turns back and pulls down his beard with a wink, and Daryl knows. He hears Mary calling his name just as he returns Santa's smile with one of his own.

Outside the stars shine brightly against the night sky, the holiday lights twinkling against the snow-covered pines surrounding Harmony Homes and the small river town of Avalon, Illinois.

Happy Christmas to all, and to all a good night.

A Taste of Avalon

Amish Friendship Bread Recipes and Tips

The holidays are a special time in Avalon. Baked goods abound in the winter months when a slice of Amish Friendship Bread, hot out of the oven, is a ready remedy to warm one's heart and soul. Here are some favorite holiday variations that have found their way into this small Illinois community.

The Amish Friendship Bread recipes included here all use 1 cup of Amish Friendship Bread starter. Detailed instructions about the starter, FAQs, and over 250 Amish Friendship Bread recipes can be found at The Friendship Bread Kitchen (www.friendshipbreadkitchen.com), home of the first Avalon novel, *Friendship Bread*.

Amish Friendship Bread Starter

Amish Friendship Bread starter is passed from one friend or neighbor to another, usually in a gallon-sized Ziploc bag or ceramic container. It's an actual sourdough starter, meaning that if you continue to feed it over time, it will become more flavorful and distinct. You can use the starter for loaves, muffins, brownies....even pancakes! If you haven't received a bag of Amish Friendship Bread starter but would like to experiment, here is the recipe for creating a starter. It'll take ten days before you are able to bake with it.

Ingredients

1 (1/4 oz) package active dry yeast
1/4 cup warm water (110° F)
1 cup all-purpose flour
1 cup white sugar
1 cup milk

Directions

1. In a small bowl, dissolve yeast in water. Let stand ten minutes.
2. In a glass, plastic or ceramic container, combine flour and sugar. Mix thoroughly.
3. Slowly add in milk and dissolved yeast mixture. Cover loosely and let stand at room temperature until bubbly. This is Day One of the ten-day cycle. You can leave in the container or transfer to a Ziploc bag.
4. On Days Two through Five, mash the bag daily (if your starter is in a container, just give it a good stir with a wooden spoon). If the bag gets puffy with air, let the air out.

5. On Day Six, add 1 cup flour, 1 cup sugar, 1 cup milk. Mash the bag.
6. On Days Seven through Nine, mash the bag daily.
7. On Day Ten, pour entire contents into a nonmetal bowl.
8. Add 1 1/2 cups flour, 1 1/2 cups sugar, 1 1/2 cups milk. Mix well.
9. Measure out equal batters of one cup each into one-gallon Ziploc bags.
10. Keep one of the bags for yourself and give the other bags to friends along with the recipe for Amish Friendship Bread (www.friendshipbreadkitchen.com). You can also freeze your starter and bake on another day.

Caleb's Amish Friendship Bread Stollen

Makes 2 loaves

Ingredients

1 cup Amish Friendship Bread starter
3 eggs
1 cup oil
1/2 cup milk
1 cup sugar
1/2 teaspoon vanilla
2 teaspoons almond extract
1 1/2 teaspoon baking powder
1/2 teaspoon salt
1/2 teaspoon baking soda
2 cups flour
1 box instant vanilla pudding
1/2 cup chopped red cherries
1/2 cup chopped green cherries
1/2 cup diced dried mango
1/2 cup chopped walnuts
Marzipan or almond paste

Directions

1. Preheat oven to 325° F (165° C).
2. In a large mixing bowl, add ingredients as listed.
3. Grease two large loaf pans.
4. Pour half of batter in greased pan lined with sugar. Lay a strip of marzipan or almond paste along length of bread. Top with remaining batter.
5. Bake for one hour or until the bread loosens evenly from the sides and a toothpick inserted in the center of the bread comes out clean.

6. Once cool, sprinkle with powdered sugar.
7. ENJOY!

Kitchen Notes

You can also make this recipe without the marzipan or almond paste addition.

Margot West's Mulled Cider

Serves 10

Ingredients

10 cups (2 1/2 quarts) apple cider
3 cinnamon sticks
3 whole cloves
1/2 teaspoon freshly grated nutmeg
1 large orange, thinly sliced

Directions

1. Place all ingredients in a large pot over medium heat and bring to a boil.
2. Reduce heat and simmer uncovered 25 to 35 minutes. Strain and serve.

Kitchen Notes

Free up your stove top by preparing and serving your mulled cider from a slow cooker.

Erin's Chocolate and Vanilla Peppermint Pinwheel Cookies

Makes 3 dozen

Ingredients

3 cups all-purpose flour
3/4 teaspoon baking powder
1/4 teaspoon salt
1 cup unsalted butter, softened
3/4 cup sugar
1 large egg, lightly beaten
1 tablespoon milk
Powdered sugar, for rolling out dough
2 tablespoons unsweetened cocoa powder
2 oz semisweet or unsweetened chocolate, melted
1 egg yolk
1 teaspoon peppermint extract
1/2 cup candy canes or peppermint candies, crushed into fine pieces

Directions

1. In a medium bowl, sift together flour, baking powder, and salt. Set aside.
2. In a larger bowl, beat butter and sugar until light and fluffy. Add in the egg, peppermint extract and milk and beat until blended. Add the flour mixture slowly until just combined and the mixture pulls away from the side of the bowl.
3. Divide the dough in half and wrap one half in waxed paper and refrigerate.
4. Whisk cocoa into the melted chocolate and add

remaining dough into mixing bowl until combined.

5. Wrap chocolate half in waxed paper and refrigerate until ready to use.

6. Preheat oven to 375° F and line cookie or baking sheets with parchment paper.

7. Remove dough from refrigerator. Sprinkle work surface and rolling pin with powdered sugar.

8. Roll each half into a rectangle about 1/4-inch thick with the vanilla dough slightly larger in size. Handle as little as possible—if the dough warms or sticks to the rolling pin, place a cold cookie sheet on top for ten minutes to chill the dough before continuing.

9. Lay the chocolate dough in the center of the vanilla dough and roll in a log beginning at the long edge. Roll the finished log in the crushed peppermints. Wrap in wax paper and refrigerate for 3 hours.

10. Unwrap dough and roll log briefly on the counter to regain the round shape. Cut crosswise into 1/4-inch slice and arrange on cookie sheets one inch apart.

11. Bake for 9 minutes until edges are lightly browned, rotating cookie sheets midway through.

12. Allow to cool on cookie sheets before transferring to wire racks to cool completely.

Kitchen Notes

Keep a cold cookie sheet in the freezer while preparing this recipe. If your dough warms or sticks when you roll it out, place the cold cookie sheet on top of the dough for 10 minutes to chill it.

You can make these cookies up to a week in advance.

Bartholomew Solomon's Cassoulet

Serves 8

Ingredients

3 cups white beans, drained
7 slices bacon, coarsely chopped
1 (4 lb) pork shoulder, cut into 1-1/2-inch cubes
1 lb kielbasa sausage, sliced into 1-inch slices
2 medium onions, chopped
6 garlic cloves, roughly chopped
2 stalks celery, chopped
2 teaspoons dried chili pepper flakes (or to taste)
2 carrots, peeled and sliced
1 tablespoon dried thyme
1 bay leaf
2 cups chicken broth
1 (14 oz) can diced tomatoes (undrained)
3 tablespoons tomato paste
1/2 cup dry white wine
Salt and pepper
1 1/2 cups coarse fresh breadcrumbs
1/2 cup parmesan cheese
1 tablespoon olive oil

Directions

1. Preheat oven to 325° F (165° C) degrees.
2. In a bowl, toss breadcrumbs with Parmesan cheese. Set aside.
3. In a large ovenproof pot or Dutch oven, sauté the chopped bacon until crisp; transfer the bacon to a large bowl. Pour off bacon fat and reserve, leaving a thin layer of bacon fat in pot.

4. Add the breadcrumbs to the pot and cook at medium high heat, stirring often, until golden and crisp, 2 to 3 minutes.
5. Transfer to a plate and set aside.
6. Add 3 tablespoons of bacon fat to the pot, then add in the pork shoulder cubes and kielbasa slices, cooking in batches. Transfer to the bowl containing the bacon.
7. Add onions, garlic, celery, carrots, bay leaf, thyme and dried chili flakes. Sauté until tender.
8. Add tomato paste, stirring for 1 minute.
9. Add chicken broth and tomatoes with juice. Bring mixture to a boil.
10. Add the pork, kielbasa and bacon, stirring to combine.
11. Cover pot and transfer to preheated oven for 1 hour.
12. After 1 hour, stir in wine and canned beans. Season with salt and pepper.
13. Top with bread crumbs and return pot to oven uncovered.
14. Cook until the pork is tender and the topping is golden and crisp, approximately 45 minutes. During baking, break the crusty top and push it into the juices 3 or 4 times.
15. Serve with a green salad or fresh bread.

Kitchen Notes

This tastes even better the next day and can be prepared a day in advance.

Flora's Rum Raisin Amish Friendship Bread

Makes 2 loaves

Ingredients

1 cup Amish Friendship Bread starter
3 eggs
1 cup oil
1/2 cup milk
1 cup sugar
1/2 teaspoon vanilla
1 teaspoon rum extract
2 teaspoons cinnamon
1 1/2 teaspoon baking powder
1/2 teaspoon salt
1/2 teaspoon baking soda
2 cups flour
1 box vanilla instant pudding
1 cup raisins in 1/2 cup rum (soak overnight for best flavor)
2 tablespoons turbinado sugar

Directions

1. Preheat over to 325° F (165° C).
2. Grease 2 large loaf pans.
3. Dust the greased pans with granulated sugar.
4. Combine all ingredients except 1 tablespoon turbinado of sugar in a large bowl.
5. Pour the batter evenly into the pans.
6. Sprinkle remaining tablespoon of turbinado sugar over each loaf.
7. Bake for 55 minutes or until bread loosens evenly from the sides.
8. ENJOY!

Kitchen Notes

Soak the raisins in rum overnight and top the loaves with turbinado sugar before baking. The granulated and turbinado sugar crystals add a delightful crunch. If serving to friends, skip the turbinado and glaze with honey, topping with a few extra raisins.

Questions for Discussion

1. Which stories were your favorite? Why?
2. In "Lemon Creams," Melvin O'Malley is upset that his daughter, Barbara, has placed him in Harmony Homes. Do you agree with her decision?
3. Who do you think the anonymous donor of the free turkeys or hams may be? Why?
4. In "Gift Wrapped," Margot West's first impression of the stranger outside her store makes her defensive–she even contemplates calling the police. What changes for her? Would the surprise waiting for her at home have changed in any way had she sent the man away?
5. The holidays are a special time for family, but Erin Meeks ("Cookie Exchange"), Joanne Stuckey ("Winterberry Wreath") and Bartholomew Solomon ("And We're Wassailing") may be spending Christmas alone. Are there times when you think you're alone but unexpectedly find yourself in the company of others?
6. What do you think will happen with Jack's letter in "Late Bloomers?" Do you think the old adage, "Time heals all wounds," is true?
7. Cooper Buck, in "Sleigh Bells," receives an unexpected

gift. What are some things you would do for yourself and others if you received a similar gift?

8. In "Scrooged," the men of the Bah Humbug Club have found small ways to make a big difference. What anonymous acts of kindness have you witnessed or experienced? Do you agree that the holidays have become over-commercialized and that we've forgotten what the spirit of the season is really about? If so, what can we do about it?

9. "Room at the Tea Salon" begins with two women, Nicole Gray and Carla Pike, uncertain about their immediate future. In a matter of hours, both of their lives have potentially changed as a result of their meeting. Do you believe a meeting like this Has anything similar happened to you?

10. The final story, "Secret Santa," brings us back to Harmony Homes. Any guesses who Santa might be? Do you think Melvin's initial prediction that Mary McLean won't last six months will hold true? How does Melvin change over these short few days?

11. *An Avalon Christmas* is dotted with food and recipes. What are some of your favorite recipes of the season?

12. In all of the Avalon books, one constant theme is how we are connected in ways both seen and unseen. Do you see these connections in your own life?

13. If you could have one holiday wish this year, what would it be? Why?

For More Information

Meals on Wheels is a national service that provides home-delivered meals for seniors and people in need. Approximately 11% of all seniors experience some form of food insecurity. To learn more about them or to donate, please visit www.mowaa.org.

For more than 250 Amish Friendship Bread recipes or to join Darien's online friendship bread community, visit the **Friendship Bread Kitchen** or join the discussion on Facebook or Twitter.

www.friendshipbreadkitchen.com
www.facebook.com/fbkitchen
www.twitter.com/fbkitchen

Acknowledgments

My heartfelt thanks to Nancy Sue Martin and Kathryn Wilkie, my early readers. Holiday hugs for my family—Darrin, Maya, Eric and Luke—who believe in the magic of the season and my capacity to tell a good story.

It is also a blessing when we discover our own angels. Here are some of mine: Frank and Christine Hustace and family, Alana Haitsuka and family, Mary Spears, Tom Hassett, Mary Embry, the Hsu and Gee ohanas, Peggy Yuan and Jason Chin and family, Deanna Lee and family, Lisa Dahm, Matilda Tompson, Joe Gaglione and family, Clinton and Nancy Gee, Jackie Hahn, Frank and Jan Morgan, Stephen Peters, Lora Schlarb and family, Dave Steiner, Olivia Tran and family, and Matthew Pearce. Priya Blair, shared her lovely name with the book—I was happy to include it. I'm also grateful to Carin Gilfry, the talented narrator of the audio book, who was both a pleasure to work with and whose voice brought these stories to life.

And my gratitude to those of you who keep me company in my virtual kitchen, the Friendship Bread Kitchen. Keep on baking!

What's Next

Please turn the page to read an excerpt from Darien's next Avalon title, *An Avalon Valentine*, available January 2015.

Chapter One

Paul Singh, U.S. Postal carrier and recent transplant to the town of Avalon, Illinois, stands on Lucy Blake's doorstep holding a small package. "Mmmm, do I smell chocolate?"

He takes a deep inhale but Lucy knows it isn't necessary. She's been in the kitchen for the past twenty-four hours and her house reeks of chocolate. *She* reeks of chocolate. It's in her clothes, her hair, her skin. It always smells like chocolate at 214 Elm Street. Not to mention there's a telltale smear of it across her otherwise white apron.

"Hi Paul," she says. "Just gearing up for Valentine's Day orders. I can't believe it's only two weeks away. When you come back tomorrow I'll have some samples ready."

"Tomorrow's Sunday," he says with a twinkle in his eye. "My day off. Will they make it to Monday?"

Lucy laughs. "Yes," she says.

He flashes her a grin and gives a small bow. "Then I look forward to Monday with great anticipation."

Lucy accepts the package, pretending to be interested in how her name is written in neat, perfect script, but really she's sneaking a look at Paul. He looks about thirty five, handsome with smooth cocoa skin and dark hair that's on the edge of being moppy. He always wears a smile, which is a huge change from the last mailman, a surly guy by the name of Walter who resented the short flight of stairs from the street to her door. And his fingernails. It may seem like a small thing but Walter had been a nail biter and it always made Lucy shudder whenever she saw him, his fingernails short and scraggly, the skin angry and red.

Paul, on the other hand, has groomed fingernails, clean and nicely trimmed. Kind of like the rest of him.

Lucy feels her cheeks pink. *Stop it,* she tells herself. She still remembers meeting him for the first time almost six months ago. After having settled from no more than a brisk nod from grumpy Walter, she hadn't been prepared to see Paul on her doorstep, handing Lucy her mail as he introduced himself. He promised to do whatever he could to make sure her mail was delivered on time and in good condition.

"Well," she'd laughed, surprised by his professionalism. "Thanks. But it's just the mail. And if you happen to lose a bill or two, it's not like I'd complain. I mean, no offense to your job or anything."

He'd held up his hands as if to say, *no offense taken,* and that's when she'd seen his ring, a smooth gold band that shone brightly. She wanted to ask about it, about his wife or if they had any kids or where they had moved from, but of course she didn't.

"It's an honor to deliver your messages," he'd continued, and she couldn't quite tell if he was serious or joking. His voice was as smooth as caramel but there was also a slight accent in his otherwise perfect English. British? European? She wasn't sure.

Now as she watches him make his way down the icy

stairs, she can't help but feel a bit wistful. She pictures him going home after a long day's work, pulling up a chair in front of a fire, a mug of hot chocolate waiting for him. Someone would put a warm blanket around his shoulders and ask him about his day. Maybe a dog or a cat curls up beside him. He'll listen to the sounds of his house—a home—and maybe there would be music on the radio, an aria drifting in the background. It suits him.

And what of Lucy? She closes the door and turns back towards her kitchen. Thirty two and still single, though not by choice. Of course that's not what she tells people. She tells them that she enjoys her solitude, her freedom, the days and nights that she gets to call her own. No one to argue or disagree with, to wait on or wait for. Her house is exactly as she likes it. Her married friends with children sometimes look at her in envy. *Look at you*, they'll say. *You still have your figure, you get sleep. You can date anyone you want or have as much peace and quiet you desire. Do you know how lucky you are?*

She wants to shake them. *Do you know how lucky* you *are?* she wants to yell, but yelling isn't what Lucy does. Instead she just smiles and nods, amazed that they actually believe someone would choose to be alone.

In the end it was chocolate that saved her, and in more ways than one. She'd been working as a copy editor for the *Avalon Gazette*, the local newspaper, and while she wasn't miserable, she wasn't happy, either. It was just a job and as hard as she tried, she couldn't make it into anything more than that. *How great it would be*, she would think, *to feel passionate about your job*. She consoled herself with the fact that if she didn't have the perfect job, at least she had the perfect fiancé.

And then Martin called off their engagement. The save-the-date announcements had just gone out—almost two hundred dollars' worth of stamps to almost five hundred people—when Martin admitted to having an affair. An affair! With a kindergarten teacher who worked at Barrett Elementary in the next town over. Lucy felt cheated, but for the oddest of reasons—for the life of her she could not summon anger against a kindergarten teacher. Why couldn't he have had an affair with his personal trainer or secretary like most men?

"You're too good for me," had been Martin's version of a pitiful apology. "I know you'll find someone else worthy of your love."

If she'd been feeling any heartbreak, it ended right there. *Too good of him? Find someone else worthy of her love?* Please. That had been the straw that broke the camel's back. Lucy decided then and there that she was over it. She was over Martin, over dead end relationships, over dead end jobs. She quit the *Gazette*, went to the Pick and Save in search of chocolate and came home with a bag full of every bar they carried. Within minutes her floor was littered with wrappers, her mouth full, but Lucy wasn't any closer to feeling the relief she'd hope for. The store-bought chocolate was terrible, no subtlety, no snap, too sweet. Instead of feeling satisfied, she felt empty.

In the end she'd gone online and ordered the best chocolate she could find. She started in Europe but ended up in South America, looking for chocolate with high-content cacao, pure and unadulterated. The best chocolate didn't need to hide behind other flavors or ingredients, didn't need to be dressed up beyond what was necessary. She swooned the first time she tried stone ground chocolate. Lucy began to collect chocolate like fine wine.

Her friends found it humorous at first. "It's just chocolate!" they'd exclaimed. Their palates were trained for artificial and sweet, for extra fillers, for the next thing to eat. They didn't know how to savor a single square on their tongue, letting it slowly melt as they took in each aroma. Delicate fruit or flower first, followed by warmer notes of roasted nuts or spices, finishing with a woody or malted note toward the end. A single square of good chocolate and a cup of earl grey could carry Lucy through the day.

To make ends meet, Lucy took freelance odd copy editing jobs, mostly online. When she helped write website copy for an artisan chocolate maker in Michigan, she knew she'd found it. She arranged to trade her work for an introduction to chocolate making. By the time the website was finished, Lucy had discovered her passion.

She continued to freelance as a copy editor by day, chocolatier at night. In fact, her first delivery of couverture chocolate was from Paul on his first day. He hasn't known her without chocolate in her life.

"Come on, Kaftan, it's time to get back to work." The grey Siamese weaves between Lucy's legs. "If we can't get this business up and running over Valentine's Day, we may as well call it quits. That means I'll have to find a real job again, and you'll go back to your lonely days. You don't want that, do you?"

Kaftan purrs and jumps onto the couch, his tail beckoning Lucy to join her. Lucy sighs—she needs to get back in the kitchen, which is off-limits to Kaftan, but she doesn't quite feel like working just yet.

Then she remembers the package in her hands.

"We got mail," she says to Kaftan. She sits down and studies the brown paper wrapping. The return address is in

Avalon, but there's no name. It's addressed to her—Miss Lucy Mallory Blake—and the handwritten script resembles fine calligraphy. She sees that it's written in black ink, not some cheap ball-point but with the texture of the nib of a fountain pen. Long tails curling across the scratchy brown paper. It looks like art, a drizzle of fine chocolate.

Her phone rings, making her jump. "I need to get out more," she tells Kaftan as she reaches for the phone. "I'm spending too much time talking to cats and getting spooked by my phone."

Kaftan responds with a flick of the tail. Lucy waves him away. "Hello?"

"Is this Lucia Blake?" comes the hurried response. "The chocolatier?"

"This is *Lucy* Blake," Lucy says. "And yes, I make chocolate."

"Thank God!" There's a whoosh of relief. "My name is Celia Love and I need to order some chocolates for Valentine's Day."

Lucy drops the package on the couch and searches for a pen and pad of paper. "I have several different-sized gift boxes to choose from," she begins, forcing her voice to sound calm. "You can choose from a mixed selection of eight pieces, twelve pieces, sixteen or twenty-four pieces of chocolate…"

"No, no. You see, I'm throwing a party for my parents. They're celebrating their fiftieth anniversary on Valentine's Day and I want favors at every plate. Can you do that?"

"Of course," Lucy says, though she's not sure that she can. She's used to making small batches, and she'll need to keep her inventory for the farmer's market and the shops around town. "We can do a single or double truffle in a small box. How many people would you need these for?"

"I don't know," Celia says. She sounds overwhelmed. "I'm putting the invite together now and I've told people about the party, but I don't have a head count. I'm asking people to RSVP within the next ten days but it's already so late. Maybe fifty?"

Lucy lets out a breath. Fifty she can do, no problem, even a hundred is fine. "Sure," she says. "I need a deposit if you decide to place the order. I can send you a price list with the different flavors and then you can pay by check of credit card. I have some small favor boxes in stock—silver, gold, black, white and of course, red."

"Oh, I'm so relieved!" Celia says. "Just send me the invoice for everything and I'll take care of it."

Lucy gets Celia's information then hangs up and looks at Kaftan. "Well," she says. "That was good luck. Our first real custom order!" She feels a trill of excitement.

Kaftan purrs, his tail swishing back and forth.

The phone rings again. Lucy knits her brows and gives Kaftan a frown. "I hope she's not canceling her order already," she says. She answers on the third ring. "Hello?"

The voice on the other end is male, smooth with a strong French accent.

"I need to place a standing order of chocolates— twenty-five dollars' worth, every day from now until Valentine's Day—to be delivered to a house in Avalon. Can you do you do that?"

She hasn't before but she'll do it for an order like this. Avalon is a small town with less than five thousand residents. It only takes a few minutes to get from one side to the other. "I can," she says, trying to keep her voice even though she wants to jump up and down. "What did you have in mind?"

He certainly knows his chocolates, Lucy thinks when she hangs up a few minutes later. He'd grilled her on her entire menu, asking about her salted caramels, the champagne truffles, her signature chocolate bark with a hint of chili. He'd scoffed at the marshmallow patty and strips of chocolate-covered bacon. In the end he'd left it up to Lucy, emphasizing that he wanted only the best and most luxurious chocolates to be delivered for the next two weeks. As a finale for Valentine's Day he bought a dozen dipped strawberries drizzled with a white chocolate finish.

"Big spender," she tells Kaftan as she makes a few final notes. The chocolate daily order is more than she made last month. "Not that I'm complaining."

There's a chime from her computer in the kitchen and Lucy rubs Kaftan behind the ears before getting up to see what it is. When she looks at the screen, she sees that the customer she just spoken with has already paid. In full.

Lucy feels a surge of hope. Not only does this mean that she might be able to afford a new chocolate enrober and move into a larger commercial kitchen, but it also means she'll be too busy on Valentine's Day to worry about the small detail that she doesn't have a valentine of her own.

"Who needs love?" she says aloud as she goes to wash her hand. Kaftan purrs, one eye open, watchful.

But as Lucy looks out the window and sees Paul greeting her elderly neighbors across the street, she wonders if it's possible. True love. Happily ever after.

"Stop it," she tells herself. It's no good, day dreaming like this. It's the stuff of fairy tales, this happily ever after.

Lucy watches Paul hand Lucia Bentley her mail, then escort her back up the walkway towards her house. Lucia

Bentley lives with her sister, Amanda, both in their seventies. As far as Lucy knows, neither of them have ever married. They seem happy enough, and yet Lucy feels it's not enough. For starters, she doesn't have a sister. And until things went south with Martin, Lucy loved the idea of a shared life, of someone to love, to trust, to grow old with, to have children with.

Maybe it's not such a stretch. The nice guys are out there—Paul is evidence of that. She just has to find one.

Chapter Two

Hannah Wang runs her bow across the strings of her cello. "G," she says. "Now you try it."

Her student, nine-year old Jacob Eammons, picks up his bow, a determined look on his face. Hannah tries not to crack a smile as he carefully lines his fingers on the bridge, then presses down. "G," he says, and proceeds to play an A.

Hannah corrects his fingering and he tries again. This time, a perfect G note sings through her small bungalow.

"I did it!" Jacob beams. "Did you hear that? That's so cool!"

"It is." Hannah smiles. "Now play it again."

The doorbell rings just as Jacob manages another perfect G.

"Wonderful!" Hannah says, standing up. She carefully leans her own cello against the stand. "Let me see who that is. Keep practicing, Jacob."

She knows her boyfriend, Jamie, is working but still she hopes he found an excuse to stop by. If he's not working his UPS route he's studying for his master's degree or driving to class, almost forty miles away. For some reason she thought they'd have more time together once he switched to a part-time work schedule, but instead he seems busier than ever.

When she opens the door she's greeted by a huge arrangement of red roses, six dozen at least. A head pokes around. "Delivery for Hannah Wang?"

"Wow!" Jacob has stopped playing and is staring at the flowers. Hannah relieves the delivery boy of the large glass vase and places it on the console by the door. "Is it your birthday?"

"No," Hannah says. She signs for the delivery and then closes the door.

"Maybe it's for Valentine's Day. My dad always gets my mom roses, but usually it's just one." Jacob bounces the bow on his knee.

Hannah wants to warn him to be careful, but she can't stop staring at the roses. They seem to overpower her small home, obscuring her reflection in the hallway mirror. *Jamie?* she wonders, but she knows it's not likely. His student loans have set him back and his supervisor put him on a shorter shift, giving him more time to study but earning less, too. Then again, maybe he received some good news. She reaches for the card tucked amongst the rose buds, closed and tight.

Ma très chère Hannah,

Tu me manques. J'étais un imbécile. Puis-je vous voir?

amour,
Philippe

The card falls from her fingers. Jacob frowns. "Are they from your boyfriend?" he asks.

Hannah can't speak, her hand covering her mouth. "No," she finally manages. She thinks what she dares not say aloud. *They're from Philippe.*

My ex-husband.

About the Author

Darien Gee is the bestselling author of six novels, including three written under the pen name Mia King. Her books have been translated in 14 languages and are selections of the Doubleday, Literary Guild, Rhaspsody and Book of the Month Club book clubs. Darien lives with her family in upcountry Hawaii. For more information, please visit www.dariengee.com.